THE RIFT IN OUR REALITY

BOOK ONE

AMY PROEBSTEL

*Blessings,
A. Proebstel*

Copyright © 2019 by Cavaliers Publishing

All rights reserved. The events, characters, and entities depicted in this book are fictional. Any resemblance or similarity to any actual events, entities, or persons, whether living or dead, is entirely coincidental. No part of this publication may be reproduced, distributed, or transmitted in any form or by any means, including photocopying, recording, or other electronic or mechanical methods, without the prior written permission of the publisher, except in the case of brief quotations embodied in critical reviews and certain other noncommercial uses permitted by copyright law. All inquiries should be submitted to amy@levelsofascension.com.

ISBN-13: 978-1-946292-35-3
ISBN-10: 1-946292-35-4

Printed in the United States of America
Cover Art by Wynter Designs

First Printing, 2019

Website: www.LevelsofAscension.com
Amazon Author Page: http://www.amazon.com/AmyProebstel
BookBub: www.bookbub.com/authors/amy-proebstel
Goodreads: www.goodreads.com/aproebstel
Facebook: www.facebook.com/levelsofascension
Twitter: www.twitter.com/amyproebstel
Instagram: www.instagram.com/amyproebstel

Dedication

This book is dedicated to the Pollman family who are blessed to have Haley in their lives every day. She is inspiring to everyone who meets her. Thank you, Melissa and Dean, for opening your hearts, family, and journey with me to share with the world.

When I asked a couple of friends for their help with this project, they were eager to jump in and come through in a big way. The first person was Lara from Wynter Designs who made the beautiful cover for this book in record time. Next was Heather Masters, a brilliant audio book narrator, who generously offered to get this book produced in her amazing style. Even with the tight deadline, she said she'd do whatever it took to make it happen. People are so good!

I'd also like to thank: Jace Slone, Delaney Wehr, Ashlynn Steiner, and Bronson. These teenagers took time out of their lives to answer the many questions I had about what's important to teenagers today. Your honesty was appreciated.

To the readers of this book, I greatly appreciate all of your kind words, amazing reviews, and support along the way. None of this would be possible without your enthusiasm for the characters and their stories.

Grab a FREE novella by Amy Proebstel

Sign up for Amy Proebstel's newsletter and grab your free copy of

Tuala's Lost Boy: Ceren's Story
A sweet paranormal romance novella.

TAKE ME TO MY FREE NOVELLA
at http://bit.ly/FMNLSU

CHAPTER ONE

I've lived an amazing life. Yet anyone on the outside might wonder why I'd think so. You see, I'm not normal. I have Batten disease. Never heard of it? I'm not surprised. Most people haven't.

If we were to compare my genetics to a card game, mine would be a hand full of jokers. But not the laughing kind. My body is unable to dispose of waste products in my brain. As the years go by, things stop working the way they should.

The first thing to go: my eyesight. Lucky for me, my parents never coddled me. If I wanted to ride my Barbie car across the front lawn, they let me go. I even rode my moped up and down the driveway.

I think it's because of them that I kept my positive attitude toward accomplishing anything I wanted. My mom always said I sparkled.

Right now, I'm working on a huge bucket list. Of course, it isn't written down; it's in my head. Nobody knows what I have planned, but that's part of the fun. Right?

I'm right in the middle of planning my epic Hood-to-Coast relay goal, when a knock sounds on my bedroom door. "Come in," I call out, scooting over to the edge of my bed. I expect it to be my mom since she's usually the only one home with me until my dad gets home from work, not to mention she's the only one who knocks so softly. "What's up, Mom?"

"Your music teacher's waiting for you in the living room," she answers.

"Shoot! I forgot all about that. I'll be ready in a second." I push myself away from the bed and reach for my bow which I keep in its special case. I don't want anything to happen to the horsehair strings, so I'm meticulous about how it's stored.

"Where's your necklace, Haley?" Mom asked suddenly.

I reached up, instantly alarmed when I only felt my bare flesh. That is until I remember I took it off while I was trying on different shirts for my starring role in my best friend's latest video. "I left it on my dresser. Can you get it for me?"

"Sure thing."

Since the sunlight is streaming through my window, I'm able to see movement in my peripheral vision. I can also smell my mother's perfume. It's my favorite scent of lilac. Her hands are as gentle as butterflies as they move my hair out of the way while she fastens the delicate chain behind my neck.

Without any conscious thought for my action, my hand raised as if to reassure myself that the little heart pendant is back in its rightful place. I already know it's there; I can feel the metal warming up against my skin.

It's really a silly piece of jewelry, but it was a gift from my best friend, Jackson, back in the first grade. I'm pretty sure he still has a crush on me, but he's always and forever only going to be my best friend.

Feeling better prepared mentally, I reach up and place my hand over my mother's where it rested lightly on my shoulder. "Thanks, Mom. I'm going to be practicing my new song today. Are you going to be listening?"

"I'm sorry, Haley. I've got some calls to return for your foundation."

I'm fairly certain she can feel my body wilt with disappointment. I'm also glad she's still standing behind me because I can't control my scowl at how she refers to the foundation created in my name. While the money raised has helped my health tremendously, I sometimes wish I could just be a normal, anonymous kid.

"Although, I have to say it's pretty soothing to hear your music in the background while I work. Maybe you can have Jackson video your session one of these times. It'd be nice to have a record of your progress. Don't you think?"

"Sure, Mom." Rather than tell her what I'm really thinking, I decided I'd better hustle out to my instructor. Besides, we both know the real reason for all the videos the family makes. It's a record that I existed.

Nobody wants to say it out loud, but there it is. We make videos to remember all the good times. Let's face it; I won't be here for too many more years. I've always known that, but each day seems more like a gift because I'm still able to do things for myself. As I said, I'm one of the lucky ones.

CHAPTER TWO

Okay, I'm done with my music lesson for the day. That was really rude how I just walked out without even telling you who I am or anything about my family. So, my name's Haley Vallem, and I'm sixteen, well, almost seventeen.

I'm the youngest in a family with four children. We've always been a close-knit family, especially since I was diagnosed with Batten disease when I was seven. From that awful day forward, we've learned to live every day in the present.

Where was I? Oh, yeah; I was telling you about my family. My oldest sister, Julia, just turned twenty-nine last week. She's married to a cool guy named Rothford...but I just call him Ross...and they have two children of their own. Don't worry, she was tested for Batten, and she isn't a carrier. Their kids are safe.

After she graduated from Portland State University with a Political Science degree...let's be honest. What was she ever going to do with that kind of degree? Anyway, she went to work as an administrator for the foundation my parents and grandparents set up in my name. She's pretty amazing at what she does; if I do say so myself!

Then there's my other sister, Rose. She's twenty-three and just out of college. She surprised my parents by becoming a drug and alcohol counselor. I think it's the perfect fit for her because she loves looking out for people and trying to help them; however she can. She ended up moving to Portland, so I don't get to see her as often as we'd both like.

Last is my brother, Hunter. He just turned eighteen, and he's chomping at the bit to move out as soon as he finishes his senior year in high school. He's supposed to be applying for colleges, but he's too busy playing video games and making movies to upload to YouTube. I'm sure he'll figure it all out, but our parents are worried.

My parents' names are Robert and Ruth. Dad owns and runs his own construction company. I'm pretty sure he's successful at it, and I know he loves driving all the big equipment. Mom used to work with his company, taking care of all the office stuff, but all that changed when I started to get sick.

Do you want to hear about it?

In the first grade, my life was completely normal. Mom even said I was reading and writing above my grade level. But that summer, my vision started to get weird. I kept having to move closer to the TV in order to be able to see it. With our busy family, nobody really noticed and I didn't say anything.

When I started second grade, it was really hard for me to keep up. My teachers complained to my parents, and that's when they took me in to get glasses. For some reason, the doctors thought those were going to help.

My vision kept getting worse throughout the year. The following summer, we visited so many doctors I lost count. One ophthalmologist even told my dad she thought I was pretending to have trouble seeing just to get attention.

Being the awesome dad that he is, he just leaned forward and said, "Respectfully, Doctor, you're wrong. I watch Haley when she doesn't know. She can't see, and something's causing it."

So, either that doctor took him seriously, or she just wanted to get rid of us, she referred us up to the Casey Eye Institute at OHSU. That September, I was put through a whole host of vision tests.

One that still makes me shiver just thinking about it was the ERG test. They put electrodes directly onto my eyeballs! Eww! They said it was necessary to test my eyes' electrical response to light-sensitive cells.

After that, we met with a specialist, Dr. Penn. He told us the worst news possible. My parents were so afraid that I was going blind. As it turned out, there was something worse than just being blind.

Now I wasn't actually there for this conversation, but I've since heard this story so many times, I feel as though I were. Dr. Penn sat across from my parents and said, "It's bad. I think she has Batten disease. It's fatal, and there's no cure or treatment."

Because Dr. Penn had diagnosed other Batten children and based on his experience, my rapid loss of sight and test results were proof positive of the disease. He was confident in his diagnosis; although, he hoped he was wrong.

In order to be one hundred percent sure of his diagnosis, he ordered a round of genetic testing for myself, Mom, and Dad. At least that time I wasn't the only one getting poked and prodded.

After three weeks of my parents having hushed conversations which would stop whenever I entered the room, we finally got the results. It was true. I had Batten disease, and both of my parents were carriers.

That's how Batten works. Because both of my parents carried the genetic defect, they had a twenty-five percent chance of passing it along to their children. Being the fourth child, I guess the odds were stacked against me.

I'll never be able to think about the fall season in quite the same way. That was when our perfect family literally fell apart. How do you face such a diagnosis without it changing how you think about your future?

From there on it was a whirlwind of finding a neurologist and other specialists I might need. Just the thing a kid wants to do to get out of school. We met with a neurologist twice. The first visit was easy; we just talked. The second time, I had to do an EEG to check if I were having seizures. I could've saved them the time by telling them I wasn't. But who wants to listen to an eight-year-old?

Next, came the mobility specialist and the low vision specialist. I didn't have any trouble getting around. They tried to get me to use a stupid cane, but I hated it. Finally, they agreed I could get along without it. Thank goodness. My vision, however, had gotten so bad now that the low vision technology really wasn't going to work for me.

I'm pretty sure my parents wanted a doctor who could

tell them what would be next and how they could prevent it. Unfortunately, that's not realistic. We simply had to wait and see. It's kind of like Russian roulette every day. What part of my body's going to stop working next? Other than my vision all but disappearing, the biggest thing to change about me is my energy level. I get tired really easy. Do you know how frustrating this is for a little kid?

I also stopped being able to keep up with everyone else when it came to the actual school work. Starting in the third grade, I went to regular school three days and the other two days a week at Montessori discovery to help me stay caught up. Over time, I discovered nobody really expected much of me. I mean, my parents still pestered me about getting my homework done, but they never said anything if I got a C on an assignment or even on a test.

My music tutor, Mr. Abernathy, introduced me to the cello. Even though the instrument is bigger than me, I just love it. Don't get me wrong, I'm terrible at getting all my practice time in, but I have fun just messing around. Mr. Abernathy keeps telling me I could play professionally if I'd just apply myself, but that just sounds like too much effort.

Besides, I've got to save some of my energy for spending time with my friends. Other than Jackson and a couple of others, my huge group of friends have disappeared. My real friends don't care that I'm blind, or that I sometimes zone out. We just have fun together.

Speaking of unconditional friends, we used to have a whole bunch of animals when I was little. We had two big dogs and two goats. They were the best. But, as with all living creatures, they grew old and eventually died. We were so busy with all my doctors' appointments, work, and my siblings' sports events that we never got around to replacing them.

My life would be truly complete if I could only convince my parents to let me get a dog. If he were trained to be a seeing-eye dog, then I wouldn't have to depend so much on my mom.

I understand that Mom wants to feel needed, but why can't she grasp that maybe I just want time by myself. Somewhere away from the house. It'd be nice to know I could walk outside and not get hit by a car.

Do you know what the worst thing about asking for a dog has been? Give up? Mom said I should learn to use that awful cane if I wanted my independence. Doesn't she get how humiliating that is? Talk about advertising my blindness to anyone who's anywhere nearby.

So now you know almost everything there is to know about me...except for one thing. Six years ago, I became one of the first CNL1 human trial subjects to receive gene replacement therapy or GRT. That's still a mouthful, so I like to call it the GReaT treatment. I was scared to do it, but it turned out to be a cinch. All they did was give me a one-time delivery of a normal copy of my defective gene. No problem.

That opportunity is the only reason I'm even able to have this conversation with you right now. Heck, who am I kidding? I'd probably be dead without it. Now you know why I think I'm so lucky. I practically won the lottery...the human trials lottery, anyway.

The GReaT treatment did slow down the progression of my disease, but it hasn't stopped it entirely. Even now, I can feel how tired my arms are just from playing the cello for an hour. Normal teenagers wouldn't have any problems with it.

In fact, I have an appointment at the hospital for later today. The researchers have requested another battery of tests to find out how far I've slipped from my previous results. Talk about depressing. Oh, well. I'll get to catch up with some of my favorite nurses.

ಸಾ ಲ್ಲಿ ಲ್ಲಿ

At least the nurse had the decency to put me in a room with another patient today. Most of the other times I'd been here, I'd be left alone with only my thoughts or an audiobook to occupy my time. I've got my earbuds in my ears, but I don't have my book turned on. I'm listening to the family talking to the little boy in the bed next to mine.

Also, the nurse had chosen my room since it had the best light coming in the windows. From my vantage point, I could keep my face forward and still be able to use my peripheral vision to see the people sitting around the boy's bed. The person closest to me appeared to be a boy about my age, maybe a little older than me.

Shoot, I think he noticed I was looking at him! I fumbled with my cell phone, attempting to get the book turned on before he calls me out for eavesdropping. Too late.

He turned to face me. "Hey, what're you in here for?"

"Just getting some tests done. What about you?" Oh man, could I have asked something any dumber? I can feel my cheeks starting to get warm, and my fingers continue to fidget with my phone.

"My brother just got diagnosed with a rare disease. They're seeing if he's a candidate for any experimental treatments."

"That sucks. I hope it works out."

"Thanks."

"What's his disease? Maybe I've heard of it."

"I'm sure you haven't. It only affects like 1:100,000 births."

"Try me."

"Batten."

My heart skipped a beat as I held my breath in pain. I already know what his family is facing. I know the hard road ahead of them. I have to answer him. "I've heard of it."

"No way. You're just saying that."

"That's why I'm here. I've got Batten as well."

"Are you sure? I mean, you're pretty old for it. Don't you think?"

A blurt of laughter escaped my mouth. I don't even know this guy, and already he thinks he's an expert on something I've been dealing with for nine years. Who does he think he is? "I think I'd know."

I'm pretty sure the boy would have continued with the conversation, but his brother's doctor arrived, and the family turned their attention to him. My nurse, Taylor, chose that moment to come and take me away. As she wheeled me past the boy's bed and out of the room, my fingers unconsciously rubbed my lucky pendant as I whispered, "Please, God, be there for this little boy."

Chapter Three

I've reached the favorite part of my school day. History class. Not only is it the last class of my day, but it also happens to be the only class I have with all of my friends. It feels more like a reunion than an actual class.

As usual, Jay has taken her seat on my right. She's really shy, to the point where you can easily forget she's in the room. Unless the teacher asks her a question about history. Then she lights up and becomes a veritable encyclopedia, amid groans of disgust from most of our classmates.

I love it, though. If Jay's talking, then I know I'm less likely to get called on. That sounds self-serving, but let's face it, I don't like studying. Jay continually offers to help me study, but I'd rather do just about anything other than think about history class when I wasn't forced to do so. Sorry, Jay!

It took me a while to figure out what it was about Jay that caused us to click so easily, considering she's my only girlfriend. One day it just hit me. She hates the idea of the future; she lives for the past. I can totally relate.

THE RIFT IN OUR REALITY

The idea of my future is something which feels like too much trouble. All of my best days have been part of my past. Each new day is more tiring than the last. But for Jay, I'm sure her future includes becoming a history professor or something along those lines.

Right behind me sits Jackson Smith. He's already just over six feet tall, so his long legs are usually stretched out. Occasionally, when I tuck my feet under the chair, they collide with his. I don't mind. He can't help it if he's so Goliath. Besides, his size might come in handy if he ends up going into the FBI when he graduates.

He's already decided on his codename. JB Smith. Well, I think we might have decided for him since he's not the only Jackson in our small circle of friends. Like all of us, he's really easy-going about the whole naming business.

We often tease him that he'll have to find undercover FBI gigs where he can sit in a car; otherwise, he won't be able to blend in with the crowd unless he investigates a basketball team.

He hates jokes about that. People always expect him to be good at basketball, just because he's tall. He prefers bowling, of all things. He's even really good at it. Someday, I know he'll figure out how to combine bowling and the FBI.

My best friend, whom you've already heard about, sits on my left. He's named Jackson O'Neil. If I have anything to say about it, he's going to be an Oscar-winning movie producer one day. After all of the movies we've produced over the years, he'll certainly have enough practice at directing unmanageable actors.

In fact, we have another production scheduled for later this afternoon. I'm sure you'll hear more about that soon enough. So, I tap my fingers impatiently on my desk as I wait for the bell to ring letting us know we're finally being released from class. My internal clock is telling me it's almost time.

My stomach let out a loud growl just as the class grew quiet. Jackson chuckled beside me. I know he's probably not the only one to have heard it.

Right on cue, JB cleared his throat and mumbled, "Nice one," from behind his hand covering his mouth. I've given up being embarrassed by such trivialities. Besides, what could I have done to prevent it?

Just as my classmates begin to laugh at my expense, the bell rings, and I'm immediately forgotten in their haste to escape to lunch. I, on the other hand, get to go home. As a group, we leave the room to put our stuff back in the lockers.

"Is Hunter ready for today's shoot?" Jackson asked, excited for the second day of cloudy weather to finish the previously abandoned shoot because of the untimely sunshine.

"I think so, but he's going to be getting home late. Dad needed his help at work right after school today."

"Oh, man! Can't he get out of it? What if the sun comes out and ruins everything? Who knows how long we'll have to wait again before we can film the final epic battle of the zombies?"

I placed my hand on his arm to console him. He easily worked himself up when his production schedule didn't go as he planned. "I'm sure he'll be fast. Speaking of which,

I've got to hustle. The bus won't wait forever for me." I shoved my books into our locker and waited for him to walk with me.

I felt him move to shut the locker, letting me know he was ready to go. As usual, he led the way, while I fell into step slightly behind him, but mostly beside him. He hated the way the other students would purposely run into me just because I couldn't see straight ahead of me.

Unlike Jackson, I never even heard their snide comments about me leaving on the 'short bus.' Although, I usually knew when something had been said because Jackson's arm would tense as he balled his hands into fists in frustration. Leaning forward, I said, "It's okay, Jackson. They're just stupid kids."

"I wish you'd let me rearrange their faces for them," Jackson muttered, mostly for himself.

He knew how I felt about violence. Besides, my reasons were purely selfish. "No way. Then you'd get suspended, and I wouldn't have anyone to keep me company."

I could feel him begin to relax as I restated my normal comeback to this perpetual problem. "Besides, Jackson, think of it this way."

"What's that?"

"I may be going on the short bus, but I'm the one leaving this place. They get to stay here for the rest of the day. So who's the special one after all?"

"You've always been special to me, Haley." Jackson's hand reached over and patted mine where it still rested on his other arm.

"I know. You're my best friend. I don't know what I'd do without you!" I knew that's not what he wanted to hear, but it was the best I could do for him. He felt like a brother to me, nothing more.

Jackson led me straight to the door of the bus.

"See you tomorrow, Jackson," the driver called out over my shoulder to my escort as I entered the bus. I knew the first seat would be vacant, as that was my designated seat. Penny, the bus driver, liked Jackson and repeatedly told me I should date him. Sometimes, I think she just liked giving me a hard time because I always blushed at this comment.

The drive home was unusually quiet. It gave me time to think about the people in my life. I kept coming back to my motley group of friends at school. We were all misfits of a sort. Jay was the quiet nerd. JB was too tall for his own good. Jackson was...well, Jackson. He caused his own drama, especially with all the videos he made of that puppet his grandmother gave him. Luckily, we finally convinced him to start making other video productions. It was starting to get weird having a fifteen-year-old playing with a hand puppet.

Then there was me. I was the blind girl. The only student with a visible disability in the school. I probably should have been transferred to the blind school, but I wanted to stay with Jackson. Then I ended up meeting our other friends.

We had our place in the school. Someone had to make up the misfit group. Why not us? At least we were good kids. That's more than a lot of other parents could say about their 'cool' kids. Our parents always knew where to find us.

It was really easy for me. I got lost simply leaving my driveway. I stayed right where I was supposed to. That is unless I had Jackson, JB, or Jay to guide me somewhere new.

I felt the bus turn onto our driveway. There was a dip in the road only on the passenger side, followed almost immediately by a couple of deep cracks which made a unique thumping sound on the tires. I pulled my jacket closer around me as I prepared for the cold air of outside.

"See you tomorrow," Penny announced, as she reached over to push the door latch open.

I heard the squeak of the rubber gaskets of the door resting against the inside frame. I stood up and answered, "See you," as I made my way down the steps.

Penny was an expert at navigating the bus. She always parked in exactly the same place, so I never had to worry about tripping over anything. I felt the walkway under my feet and walked the thirteen steps to the front door.

I let myself in and then heard Penny rev the engine to leave. She always made sure I made it inside before she left. She insisted it was because of the liability, but I think it's because she loves the kids she drives home. I think of her as extended family. She's pretty cool.

The house was quiet, which was a good thing. As exhausted as I felt, I knew a nap was the first task on my afternoon agenda right after I ate lunch. Knowing the grueling production schedule Jackson had planned for this evening, I was going to need all the rest I could get if I were going to play my part even half-way convincingly.

ಖ ೦ಙಖ ೦ಙ

The side of my bed dropped down alarmingly. I groaned as I realized my nap was officially over. "Is it that time already?"

"Yep. Time to get up, sleepyhead. I've already got everything all set up outside. All by myself, I might add."

"Hunter's not home yet?" I sat up, pushing my unruly hair out of my face.

"He just got here. He's getting changed as we speak."

"Well, that's good. I'd hate to have to deal with your rotten mood if we couldn't get this filmed today."

"Very funny. Come on; I've got to get your makeup on. The light's perfect outside. We've got to hurry."

ഊ ഗ൞ഌ ൙

"And cut!" Jackson called out just before letting out a whoop of happiness.

I smiled at his enthusiasm. This was the reason I went along with all his crazy schemes. I loved making him happy.

"That was our best production ever," Hunter practically yelled in his excitement.

"Totally awesome!" Jackson agreed.

I heard a loud crack and assumed Jackson and Hunter were congratulating themselves with a high five. I rolled over onto my side from where I'd been 'murdered' on the grass in the final epic scene of the zombie apocalypse. The fake blood was drying all over my body, and I felt disgusting.

"You know, I sure miss making the talent shows and fashion exhibits," I called out to them. I knew they would have some snide comments to make about that.

"Come on! This was so epic," Hunter argued.

"As far as I can see, this film only had one advantage over those original ones." I stood up, facing where I'd last heard the boys.

"Yeah; what's that?" Hunter challenged.

I lifted my arm to my mouth and took a long lick of the fake blood made up of colored chocolate syrup. I smirked as I heard the gagging sounds from the boys. That was my cue. "This makeup tastes much better." I chuckled as I left the boys to take care of the equipment while I went inside to take a desperately needed shower.

CHAPTER FOUR

I used to think I had bionic hearing because of my sight loss. But I've learned from Hunter that I'm not the only one who can hear my parents fighting. Don't get me wrong, it's not very often, but it's still sad when it happens.

Whenever my parents go down to the basement for 'adult conversations' we know it's usually about one of us. Tonight it's my turn; not anything I've done in particular, more because of me. I lean over the vent near the head of my bed to catch it all.

"That stupid insurance company denied Haley's tests again! How do they expect us to come up with that kind of money every time the researchers need another sample?" Mom said, her voice rising throughout until she almost yelled at the end.

"We'll make it work, hon. Don't worry," Dad replied, his voice low and harder to hear.

"Don't worry? That's your solution? Where's this money supposed to come from? Did you see how much they're charging us? It's insane!"

"I'll just have to take on more clients."

"That just means you'll be spending more time away or we'll have to spend money on hiring more workers. Either way, we're still not going to have enough by the time this bill is due."

"Then I'll ask my dad for help."

"I don't want to ask him for help. This's our problem, not his!"

"I think you need a time out," Dad said.

I already knew where this was going, so I wasn't surprised when Hunter came into my room and sat down beside me on the bed.

He put his hand on my knee and said, "This isn't about you, Haley."

I didn't want to be consoled. Here Mom was getting a time out simply because she was scared about our finances. Time outs were only given when the other person thought something might be said which would be regretted later or when they needed to calm down before continuing the discussion. This *was* because of me. I shook my head and said, "They're arguing about paying for the tests I had to take. How is this not about me?"

"It's about the insurance companies."

"Yeah, because of me. I hate all of this!" I couldn't stay seated any longer; I had to move. I began pacing my room until my foot crunched down on the hair clip I must have dropped. "Ouch, ouch!" I cried out, picking up my foot and rubbing the tender spot right in the middle.

Hunter knelt and retrieved the offending clip. I could feel him next to me as well as smell the cologne he liked to drown himself in.

"Do you think I'll ever be done with all these tests?" I returned to my bed, already tired from my little outburst. I rested my ankle on my knee as my fingers continued to knead the sore spot.

"Actually, yes. I heard Mom talking on the phone with the research lab. They're in the final stages of the gene replacement therapy. They think you're the perfect candidate for it. That's why they needed this latest round of scans to be sure."

"Gene replacement therapy. I've had that done once already, but I'm still not better."

"Well, you're still alive. Besides, technology has improved a lot in the last six years. All the money your foundation has raised has made a huge difference."

"I wish some of that money could've helped with my medical bills."

"Our parents have the money."

"You mean they used to. It's getting harder and harder for them to cover everything."

"Don't worry."

"You sound like Dad."

"Really? Cool. I think that's the nicest thing you've ever said to me."

"Ha. Ha." I was just about to add more, but then I heard the front door slam. Only one person did that around here, and he wasted no time getting to my bedroom.

"Hey, did you know there're people moving into the Peterson's old house?" Jackson asked, not bothering to see if he were interrupting.

"No, but I noticed they took down the 'For Sale' sign last week. Did you get a look at who the new people are?"

Hunter asked.

"Not really. But I think they're old because I saw them moving a hospital bed in through the front door."

"Great," Hunter sighed, clearly disappointed. "I'm going to go edit some videos in my room. See ya."

"What's wrong with him?" Jackson asked, coming to sit beside me on my bed.

"He's just bummed because Mom and Dad are fighting about my medical bills again."

"Oh. That sucks. Hey, are you about ready to go? We don't have much time."

"What time is it?"

"Almost seven. Sorry, I got stuck in traffic."

"Good grief! Why didn't Hunter mention anything when he was talking to me?" I stood up, trying to remember what I was wearing. Not that it really mattered much what I wore to the support group meeting.

"You look fine. C'mon; let's get out of here. Your sandals are at two o'clock."

Jackson always made it so easy to forget I was almost completely blind. I never had to teach him how to be helpful; it just came to him like second nature. Using his direction, I unerringly grabbed my sandals and slipped them on.

Feeling rushed, I said, "Fine by me. Although, I think you just want another chance to gawk at the Peterson's house. You're probably hoping for a pretty girl to move in so you can flirt with her." I couldn't help teasing him; he just made it way too easy.

"Yeah. You know me; the player for sure."

Jackson grabbed my arm and pulled me out of the house

and into his big Ford truck. As soon as he started the engine, he turned up the radio. He clearly didn't want to talk. Maybe I'd gone too far with the girl joke.

The silent ride gave me plenty of time to contemplate the night's entertainment. I hated going to the support groups, but I did it to make my parents happy. They seemed to think it'd help me if I talked with other kids with terminal illnesses. It didn't.

As it was, I usually spent the entire hour sitting by myself. Heck, even Jackson wasn't willing to sit through all the torment. I listened to everyone's stories, even though I'd heard them all before. Hey, I said I'd go to the meetings; I never said I'd participate. Besides, I wasn't like them. I planned on living.

There was one bright point of this meeting: the announcement that this would be the last one for six weeks. I have to fight to withhold my grin of delight. With the end of the school year, the group decided to take some time off so that families could take vacations.

My guess is that the coordinator wanted to leave town for a while. In any event, the reprieve from the depressing meetings seemed like a blessing from above, and I wasn't about to argue against it.

Even better, the group coordinator let us leave early. I went outside to sit on the front steps in the sunshine. Because of the change in plans, Jackson would have no idea that he needed to come to get me so soon. I didn't bother calling him, either.

There were so few times where I could just be alone with my own thoughts – outside of the house, that is. There was no way I was giving up this time. I planned on taking full advantage of this new-found moment of freedom.

My back rested against the stair rail as my feet tapped on the step below me in rhythm to a tune I was devising. So involved had I become in the working of my new song, I failed to notice the sun no longer warmed my face. When a boy's voice spoke, I startled badly, hitting my head on the railing behind me.

"Ouch!" I cried out, my hand immediately rising to inspect the tender area on my scalp.

"I'm so sorry, I didn't mean to startle you," the boy said, his voice sounding worried as it came closer to my face. "I thought for sure you saw me."

I had to laugh at his innocent statement, even as I wracked my brain trying to place where I'd heard his voice before. "I'm sorry. Do I know you?" I asked, tilting my head in the direction I imagined he knelt.

"Yeah. Don't you remember me?"

I shook my head even as I heard the scuffing of his shoes and rustling of his clothes as he settled himself on the step beside me. "Your voice sounds familiar. Remind me again how you know me?"

"Well, I don't really know you, but we met at the hospital. My brother, Jimmy, has Batten disease. My name's Matt."

I'm pretty sure my expression just froze on my face. This was the guy I was flirting with at the hospital. Then it dawned on me that he didn't realize I was blind, well nearly blind. If he would move out of my sunlight, I might have a chance to get a better look at him using my peripheral vision, blurry as it might be.

"Aren't you going to shake my hand?" Matt asked, his voice sounding playful.

"Oh, I'm sorry," I replied, raising my hand too fast and totally bungling any chance of looking at all graceful. Yet, it did create the perfect opportunity for Matt to grab my hand in both of his as he halted my flailing motion. Was it crazy that I felt a thrill of excitement at just his touch? I must be truly pathetic to think of a simple handshake as any kind of flirting.

"Careful, there. You about took out my eye," Matt teased.

A nervous giggle escaped my mouth. Really? Did I just giggle? I tried to compose myself. "Sorry. I think you just startled me."

"I didn't catch your name."

"Probably because I never told you. I'm Haley." Unfortunately, he must have decided he didn't need to keep holding my hand now that he knew my name. I already missed the feeling. My fingers curled into a fist like I was trying to keep the memory of his touch on my skin.

"What're you doing out here all alone?"

"Oh, my meeting finished early so I thought I'd sit in the sunshine while I wait for my friend to pick me up."

"Do you need a ride? I'm parked just over there. I could take you home."

I wanted to melt right there. This was the first time a guy had ever offered to take me anywhere. More than anything, I wanted to say yes and go with him immediately. But I knew that would be wrong. Besides, Jackson was probably already on his way, and that would be beyond rude to stand him up.

I shook my head sadly. "I'm sorry," I managed to say, even though every fiber of my being wanted to jump up and run away with him. Okay, that might be a tad bit dramatic, but I was excited!

"Haley!" Jackson called from down the street.

I scowled in his direction. It wasn't like him to call out to me. He must have seen me talking with Matt. I could only assume he was trying to tell Matt that I was his, as stupid as that was. Jackson already knew I only thought of him in a brotherly way.

"Oh, is that your boyfriend?" Matt asked.

Was that jealousy I heard in Matt's tone? "No, he's just my best friend."

"Well, I should get going. See you around, Haley."

No! Matt was leaving, and I wasn't ready for him to go. I needed to think of something fast. "Hey, um, maybe I should get your phone number or something." Matt stayed quiet, so I added, "So we can talk about your brother's condition if you want, I mean."

"Oh, sure. Do you have a phone? I can put my number in there."

I fumbled with my pants pocket to get the blasted phone out before Jackson could ruin my chance. Of course, I would have been wearing my tightest pair of jeans which made it nearly impossible to get anything in or out of my pocket. Almost desperate, I stood up and managed to pull it out, but not in time.

"Hey, Haley. Didn't you hear me calling for you?" Jackson asked, his voice breathless like he'd been hurrying.

"Yes. I'm sorry, Jackson. Hey, this's Matt. We met at the hospital. His brother has Batten, too." I held out my phone, hoping Matt had stayed by my side. Apparently, I got it wrong since I felt Jackson push my hand to the side.

"She's blind," Jackson pointed out.

Ugh, sometimes I just wanted to kill Jackson. Why did he have to say that? I felt the phone being taken out of my hand. Matt's fingers brushed against mine, but the silence seemed to weigh heavily down on the three of us.

Just a few seconds later, Jackson handed my phone back to me. I could tell the difference in the feel of his hand immediately. My frown must have tipped Matt off because he started talking too fast for casual conversation.

"I'm sorry, Haley. I didn't realize you couldn't see me. I just, um, I'm sorry. See you around." His voice sounded far away as he said the last bit.

Not caring who saw me, I hauled off and whacked Jackson's arm. "Why don't you just get a megaphone to announce my blindness? What were you thinking?"

"I'm sorry. Did I mess up something with Romeo?"

"Don't start with me, Jackson." I gave myself a time out to stop myself from saying anything I might regret later. In a calmer voice, I changed the subject. "You're here early."

"Not early enough," Jackson mumbled.

Of course, I heard him, although he probably didn't think I could. I took his arm so he could lead me back to his truck and asked, "What're we filming tonight?"

Just as I knew he would, Jackson brightened up immediately. "I thought maybe we could do a production with your cello. Didn't your mom say she wanted to do a sequence on that?"

"She did. Plus, I was just thinking up a new song while I was waiting for you." With practiced ease, I pulled myself up into the seat of the truck. "Maybe you could do a video series about the birth of a new song. You know, start-to-finish progression to the finished song."

"I like it!" Jackson shut the truck's passenger door and quickly went around the vehicle to get into the driver's side.

"I knew you would." I couldn't stay mad at Jackson; it wasn't like Matt wouldn't have figured out I was nearly totally blind. Besides, I think Matt still gave me his phone number. Maybe I could have Hunter help me call him after Jackson went home. You know; to talk about his brother's illness.

Chapter Five

It's been a week since the day I met Matt again outside the group meeting. I've waffled back and forth on what I should do with the number he put in my phone. Did he just give it to me out of pity, or does he want me to call him? If it's the former, then I'd feel really stupid calling him. If it's the latter, then maybe I've waited too long to call him already.

During times like these, I really wished I could've had a close girlfriend to talk it over with. As it is, school let out for summer break two days ago, and now I don't even have Jay to talk to. Not that she'd know anything about it either; I doubt she's ever even talked to a boy other than in our group.

As if my oldest sister had radar for my problem, Julia knocked on my door before letting herself in. "Hey, Haley. What's with the sad face? Do you want to go out to dinner with me tonight?"

"I'm just thinking," I automatically answered. Almost instantly, my mood brightened. How come I hadn't thought about talking this problem over with Julia? I flung my legs over the side of my bed and tossed my ear buds over onto my nightstand. "I'd love to go. I'll be ready in five minutes!"

Julia laughed at my reaction. I knew she was only trying to get me out of the house because of something our parents had planned, but I also had an ulterior motive in mind. I ran a brush through my unruly, thick hair and pulled a hairband off of my wrist to wrap it around my ponytail. I vaguely remembered what I was wearing, and figured it would be good enough for wherever we decided to go. I turned and asked, "Do I look okay?"

"Perfect. Let's go."

"You don't have to ask me twice." I walked confidently through our house, waiting at the front door for Julia to lead me to her car. As we're driving to the restaurant, I decided now would be as good a time as any to ask her advice. "Do you think a week is too long to wait to call a boy?"

"Haley Vallem, do you have a boy you haven't told me about? When did this happen? And why is this the first I'm hearing about it?"

I knew Julia was teasing me, but I could feel the blush warming my cheeks anyway. "You and Mom have been so busy planning for going to that conference; I didn't want to interfere."

"Oh, Haley; I've always got time for my favorite little sister."

"Besides, I don't think it's all that serious." My fingers fiddled with the time-worn edges of my necklace. Maybe I was just overthinking all of it. I was beginning to wonder if this was a good idea anyway.

"Why don't you let me be the judge of that? Start from the beginning and don't leave anything out."

This was definitely new territory for both of us. I've never been interested in a boy, and she's never asked me about boys. Maybe we were both afraid I would never live long enough to get to this point, so why bother bringing it up?

With a lot of prompting and questions from my sister, I told her everything. In the end, I held my phone up and said, "So I'm not actually sure he left me his number. Nor do I know if I should call him."

Julia parked the car in front of the restaurant. At almost the same time, she took the phone from my hand. "Why didn't you ask Mom or Hunter to help you with this?"

"Really?" I asked, the sarcasm practically dripping from my mouth. "Mom would give me the third degree about how dangerous boys are and Hunter would just threaten to kill anyone who dared to speak to me."

"Okay, you've got a good point. So, I see he did actually leave you a real number. Let's call him now and see what he's up to."

Fear instantly overwhelmed me. "NO!" I yelled, too loud for the close confines of the car. In my excitement, I almost broke the chain of my necklace since I tended to fiddle with it when I was feeling uncertain or anxious.

"Don't tell me you're afraid of a simple phone call. You've never been afraid of anything in all your life."

"That's not true; I've never like scary movies."

"Says the girl who played the lead role in Jackson and Hunter's latest zombie apocalypse movie."

"That's just us messing around. None of it was real.

Besides..."

"Besides what? What can you possibly say to convince me not to press this little button to send the call?"

I felt myself practically deflate as the most troubling question finally came spilling out of my mouth. "What if he doesn't really like me in that way?"

"Would it be so terrible to just be his friend? I mean, all of your friends are guys; so how is this any different?"

She had a point. Maybe I was putting too much emphasis on the potential relationship angle. It wasn't like he was hurting for friends or anything. I'm sure this was just a casual thing for him, now that I thought about it for a second.

In a moment of weakness, I nodded my approval. The next thing I knew, Julia was shoving the phone up to my ear. At least she didn't plan on having the phone on speaker so she could be witness to a potentially embarrassing conversation.

"Hello?"

Just hearing Matt's voice caused my pulse to race and my mind to go completely blank. Julia must have heard him answer because she started jabbing me in the arm to say something back. Almost dropping the phone, I fumbled to get a better grip as I breathlessly said, "Matt? This's Haley."

"Well, hi. I was wondering if I was ever going to hear from you. What's up?"

"Um. Not much really. My sister and I are just getting ready to eat dinner. I thought I'd call to see if you gave me your real number."

I clapped my hand over my mouth. Did I really just

speak that last part out loud? What would possess me to say something so stupid?

Matt laughed as if I'd said something hilarious. At least he didn't sound offended. "It's me, all right. Do you want to hang out sometime?"

"Sure. That sounds like fun. Only…" I wracked my brain trying to explain how I don't have much freedom from home without sounding like I'm a little kid.

"I could come to your house and hang out," he offered.

Could this be real? Did he just offer to come over to be with me? I felt like pinching myself as a huge grin broke out on my face until his next words came through the call.

"I've got lots of questions for you about my brother's disease." His tone didn't change. This must have been his plan all along.

"Yeah, sure. Do you have something to write down my address?" My voice had fallen flat as my hopes for a relationship with Matt were dashed before they could actually blossom into anything that mattered.

"I'll text it to him," Julia offered, speaking loudly enough for Matt to overhear. "We should probably head inside and get a table."

She must have decided to take pity on me. I'm sure my relief was evident on my face.

"Sounds like you're busy. Go ahead and text me and we'll figure out a good time later. Have a good dinner. Thanks for calling."

Matt hung up first.

"That went awful," I said flatly as I handed the phone back to Julia. I felt a sick feeling in my gut. I heard her fingers tapping on the screen of my phone, so I guessed she was sending the text.

"What'd he say to you? Should I offer to hurt him for you? I haven't hit send yet."

"Don't you dare!" I should've known she was only baiting me. When I heard her chuckling, I had to smile in return. "He just said he wanted to talk about his brother with me."

"Of course he would. Were you thinking he was going to ask you to marry him?"

I could feel the blush overtaking my cheeks at her comment. Of course, I knew it was outrageous, but a girl could dream. He could be my knight in shining armor, right? Apparently, I'd been listening to too many romance audiobooks because it was clouding my reality for real relationships.

Julia kept talking, "Besides, he's probably just as nervous about seeing you as you are him. He only said what came to his mind. Kind of like you did at the beginning of the conversation. I think I may need to give you some lessons on how to talk to a guy. C'mon. Let's go eat."

ဆ ෬ജ ൙

"Is it always that hard?" I asked suddenly, the French fry suspended between my plate and my mouth.

"Talking to a boy for the first time?"

I nodded.

"Every time!" Julia laughed, probably at my reaction. "Don't worry, though; it's all better from there."

"Thank goodness. I'd hate to think it could get worse."

"Well, I guess it could. But if you'll take my advice, then you'll be just fine."

"What's your sage advice?"

"Be yourself. Don't try to read anything into your conversations with him. Be his friend."

"Ugh. Now I know how Jackson has felt all these years."

"He brought that on himself."

"What makes you say that?"

"Really? What self-respecting girl is going to want to go out with a boy who made videos of his puppet? You're lucky you didn't have to watch them."

"They couldn't be that bad. You're just trying to mess with me." I grinned at her attempt to cheer me up.

"Not kidding. Just ask Hunter. I think the best thing that ever happened to Jackson was having Hunter get him to work on some better video projects. Now Jackson's got a shot of having a future in the film industry."

This time I really did laugh. "Remind me to thank Hunter when we get home."

"Not a chance. Our brother doesn't need any encouragement for his ego."

"What're you talking about? He's as sweet as pie."

"Maybe to you. He's always adored you."

"He can't help it if I'm his favorite." Maybe now was as good a time as any to ask the other thing bothering me. "What're you and Mom working on? I mean, every time I come into the room, the two of you get really quiet."

"You're too perceptive for your own good. But you don't have anything to worry about."

"That makes me worry more!"

"Not this time. We're planning to make a couple stops in

Northern California on our way down to the research conference this year. You know, you could come with us if you wanted to."

Just the idea of it made me want to jump up and run screaming out of the restaurant. Shaking my head wildly, my ponytail hitting the sides of my face with my intense reaction, "Nope! Not a chance. I live with Batten. I don't have any desire to be surrounded by people who're talking about how hard it is to live with people with the disease."

"It's not all about that, and you know it. There're lots of great researchers who attend it. We get to hear all about the progress they've been making in finding a cure."

"I'll start caring when they're scheduling my appointment to receive the cure. Until then, I'll live in my little bubble of loneliness."

"Maybe this summer Matt will be there to keep you company," Julia said, her voice sounding playful.

I liked the sound of that. Could I let myself believe it might be a possibility? Of course! How else was I supposed to cross that goal off of my bucket list?

CHAPTER SIX

My pulse quickened as I heard the special ring tone I'd had Julia set up for Matt's number. He was calling me! Maybe it would've been easier if his number rang like all the other spam phone calls; I might have been faster to answer it.

On the third ring, I made up my mind to take the call. No matter what happened, I could be a good friend to him, if nothing else. Besides, what harm could it be to merely talk to him?

"Hello?" I answered.

"Haley? This's Matt."

"I know. What's up?" I inwardly groaned at my dumb answer. My mind rapidly tried to recall Julia's advice on talking with boys. Oh, yes. Be myself. No problem there.

"You know, we just moved here," he started.

This was news to me. Of course, I didn't know anything about him other than his brother's illness. "Wow. Really? Where'd you move from?"

"Red Bluff, California."

"Wow, that's cool. What made you guys move?"

"Dad got a job transfer with the Bureau of Land Management. Plus, it was closer to a good research hospital for Jimmy."

"That makes sense. I was wondering why I'd never run into you at school before."

"Yeah, I'll be starting my senior year at Sprague this coming year."

"Wow, that's where I go to school. Although, I'll only be a junior."

"That's not the only thing we have in common," Matt taunted cryptically.

A smile played across my lips as I realized Matt was flirting with me; at least I thought it felt like flirting. Taking the bait, I asked, "What else?"

"I put your address into MapQuest and discovered we're practically neighbors."

"No way. Seriously? Where do you live?"

"Only about five houses away from you, actually."

"Wait! Did you move into the Peterson's old house?"

"I'm not sure, the last name sounds familiar, but I didn't have anything to do with the purchase."

"Oh, of course not. That's really cool, though." What else could I say to that? Hey, do you want to come over and hang out? No way! That would make me sound too desperate.

"Maybe we could hang out this afternoon?" Matt suggested.

If I hadn't been lying down on my bed, I might have fallen over. He had literally taken the words right out of my head. Yet, he didn't sound desperate to me. It was entirely possible I was putting too much pressure on myself over every little detail.

"What do you think?" Matt asked.

Oh, no! I left him hanging while I got lost in my own head. "YES!" Good grief, calm down girl. "I mean, that sounds fine. Do you want to come over to my house? It might be easier."

"Yeah, our house is pretty much in shambles with all the moving boxes. It'll be a relief to get away from all of it for a while. How about I come over there at one?"

"Sure. That sounds perfect."

"See you then."

Matt had a disconcerting habit of abruptly disconnecting the call. I guess that was better than the alternative of trying to decide who was going to hang up first. I held the phone clutched tightly in my hand, my heart still racing with the idea of meeting up with Matt again.

Now, if only I could figure out a way to get rid of Hunter for a few hours. Then I could have the perfect afternoon. As it was, Mom, Dad, and Julia were set to leave on their road trip in about an hour, so that would take care of the majority of people who would have an issue with Matt's appearance at the house.

What was I thinking? I didn't know Matt from Adam. He could be some deranged stalker, and here I was planning how I could get time alone with him. Was I really getting that desperate?

"Yes," I spoke aloud as I grabbed my necklace and worried the edges as I considered my alternatives.

"I know that look, Haley. What's going on?" Julia asked from the other side of my room.

I started at the sound of her voice. It wasn't often that people could sneak up on me. I bit my bottom lip and sat up a little straighter on my bed. "Do you think we could talk privately?"

"Sure."

I heard the soft clicking of my door latching shut before Julia's weight shifted the angle of my mattress as she sat down near the foot of the bed. "Does this have something to do with Matt?"

The corners of my mouth tipped up, and I'm sure I blushed as I nodded silently.

"I thought I heard his ring tone when I was talking to Mom. What did he say?"

"Good grief, what else did you hear?" I never thought about anyone eavesdropping on my conversation. This could get really bad.

"Nothing. Don't worry. Nobody paid any attention to the sound, especially with all the video noises usually coming out of Hunter's room. I only noticed it because we set it up yesterday."

I let out a sigh of relief, which was silly considering I'd technically done nothing wrong. "He's coming over here at one. What should I do?"

"Be yourself. Remember?"

"Right. I've got that down. I mean, what should we talk about?"

"Ask him about himself. I'm sure he'll do the same with you. Just get to know one another. Before you know it, the two of you will be like you are with Jackson."

"Eww. I hope not!"

"No, I just mean it'll be easy to hang out together. No expectations, no awkwardness."

"Okay, I can go for that." I set my phone down on my nightstand and sat up a little straighter. Pushing my hair behind my ears, I asked, "When're you guys leaving?"

"If I didn't know better, I'd say you were trying to kick us out already."

"Maybe a little," I grinned as I replied.

"I like seeing you happy like this, Haley. I already think Matt's a good influence on you."

"Now, if only you can convince Mom and Dad of that while you're gone."

"I really wish you would've decided to come with us. We don't normally go as a road trip. It would've been like old times."

"I know what you mean. That part did have me a little tempted, but then I thought of the ultimate destination, and I just couldn't bring myself to say yes. You can tell me all about it when you get home. I always enjoy the way you describe everything anyway because you make it seem like I was there with you."

"I'm glad. Ever since you were diagnosed, I began to see the world differently. I wanted to give you the details you were missing. And then I discovered I enjoyed everything so much more because I paid better attention. Thank you for that, Haley."

"Well, that's my job in the family. It's nice to be appreciated." I polished my knuckles on my shirt in a teasing manner.

Julia swatted my feet playfully before she said, "I should probably get back to packing the car. I'm sure you want us hitting the road sooner rather than later." She stood up from the bed and walked across my room. I heard the handle of my door rattle when she said, "Maybe I'll put together a grocery list for Hunter to go get this afternoon. I'm pretty sure you're getting low on food."

I couldn't help grinning at her perfect scheme. Nothing stirred Hunter more than the promise of food. As long as he used someone else's money, he had no problem going to the store to get it. What can I say? I've got the best sister.

80 CB80 CR

I'm pretty sure Hunter knew something was up with me when he came and told me he was leaving to go grocery shopping. Even though I tried to act casual, I practically shoved him out the front door in my haste to get him gone. I leaned against the inside of the door, my heart hammering wildly at what I was about to do.

My phone just chimed with the fifteen-minute alarm I'd set to warn me of Matt's visit. I don't think Hunter heard it, but he could hardly miss my jittery attitude. You'd think I was planning something illegal with how amped up I was getting. I'm sure no girl ever went through quite this much at the prospect of a boy coming over.

This was momentous. It was quite possibly the start of something quite huge for me. What if Matt were 'the one' for me? Good grief, get a hold of yourself. He's not coming over here to propose or anything, I reminded myself.

Just as I pushed myself away from the door, a knock sounded. A squeal of fear escaped my lips. Who could be knocking? Surely Matt wouldn't dare to be fifteen minutes early. Could he?

I rested my hands on the door, leaning forward, I called out, "Who is it?"

"Matt," he announced.

Yep. Definitely him. I guess I wasn't going to get as much time to get myself worked up with nerves as I thought. It was probably for the best. I reached for the handle and swung the door open. "You're early," I stupidly said.

"Yeah, I saw that guy drive away so I thought I'd take a chance."

"That was my brother, Hunter."

"Oh, good. I was hoping it wasn't someone else I should be worried about." He suddenly stopped talking and cleared his throat nervously.

"It's such a nice day. Do you want to walk around the yard together?" I asked. I got the distinct impression he was just as nervous as myself. For some reason, that seemed to help calm me. Without waiting for an answer, I stepped outside, my side brushing against Matt's.

"Sorry. I keep forgetting you're blind."

"Good. I don't want that to be the first thing people notice about me."

"Well, you do a good job of hiding it."

I smiled. "To be honest, I'm not completely blind. I just can't see anything directly ahead of me. I can see shapes and colors with my peripheral vision, especially in really bright light."

"Really? So if we went into the sunshine, you'd be able to see me?"

"Yep."

"Do you want to do that?"

"I'd like to if you don't mind."

"Not at all."

"Well then, lead me to the best patch of sunlight." I put my hand out the same as I would with Jackson, forgetting that Matt might not know what I needed. Apparently, the gesture was universal because Matt tucked my hand onto his arm and began walking off the porch with me in tow.

I probably didn't need the assistance; I'm well-acquainted with my entire property. But I sure liked having his physical contact. Not liking the silence growing between us, I asked, "Did you walk over? I didn't hear your car pull up."

"Yes. We really are close neighbors. I hope you don't mind."

"Not at all." We came to a stop at one of my favorite places in the yard, and I could feel the sunshine warming my hair. "This really is the best time of day for my sight. The sun is almost directly overhead, so it doesn't shine directly into my eyes." I kept my hand on his arm, and I turned my body, so I was parallel to him. "You're taller than I thought. Would you mind leaning down a bit?"

As soon as he did as I asked, I leaned in closer to his face. I probably should have mentioned how close I'd have to get to really see any details of his features, but where's the fun in that. I could feel his breath on my cheek and saw that his eyes were a beautiful shade of blue, the same as the afternoon sky on a summer's day.

"What's going on here?" Hunter asked.

Matt and I both guiltily jumped away from one another. I turned to the direction of his voice and asked, "What're you doing home?"

"Get away from my sister!" Hunter said.

I heard a small grunt from Matt and realized Hunter must have pushed him. "Stop it, Hunter. I invited him over. We weren't doing anything wrong."

"It didn't look like that from what I walked up on. It looked like you two were making out."

More than mortified, I stammered to reply. My hands clutched into fists as I wished my brother would drop dead where he stood. Why would he say something so…so embarrassing? Luckily, Matt spoke up on my behalf.

"You're Hunter, right?" Matt asked, his voice calm and reasonable.

"Yes. And just exactly who are you and what're you doing over here with my sister?"

"My name's Matt Dietrich. My family just moved into the house down the street. But Haley and I actually met at the hospital a couple of weeks ago."

Well, that was something new. I hadn't thought to ask for his last name yet. At least Hunter's interruption was slightly rewarding, if unexpectedly rude and humiliating. "Yes, and Jackson met him last week after my group meeting."

"Hmph."

I could just imagine the stare-off between the two boys. Hunter had this misplaced need to protect me. It was about time I set him straight. "I asked Matt to let me see him. We weren't doing anything wrong."

THE RIFT IN OUR REALITY

I don't know what look passed between the boys, but my answer must've satisfied Hunter because his attitude changed immediately. "Sorry about that, man. I just have to look out for my little sister."

"You're not my father, Hunter. Don't you have some grocery shopping to get done?" This was my worst nightmare coming to life. What was Hunter going to do next? Offer to be my chaperone?

"It can wait. Besides, there's no way I'm leaving you here alone. I'll go after Matt leaves."

CHAPTER SEVEN

As it turned out, having Hunter hanging out with us did make getting to know one another much less stressful. We ended up all going to the grocery store, with the idea of getting Matt used to the layout of the town. I just enjoyed sitting next to him in Hunter's truck.

By the time Matt left for the night, it was already after eleven o'clock. The day couldn't have gone any better. And, I'm pretty sure Hunter really likes Matt. They seemed to bond over some video game they both like to play.

I wandered off to my bedroom, already more exhausted than I've been in a long time. It seemed like too much trouble undressing for bed, so I opted to flop down on the comforter while I could recoup enough energy to change into my pajamas.

Hunter stopped at my open bedroom door and said, "He's pretty cool, Haley. I like him."

I shook my head in the dark room. I suppose I should be glad Hunter liked him; it'd make seeing him again much easier. Yet, I couldn't help teasing him. It was the least I could do for him initially humiliating me in front of Matt.

"Do I hear a bromance blooming?"

"Ha. Ha. Not likely. I'm heading to bed."

"Night," I replied, a yawn catching me off-guard. Just as I suspected, Hunter immediately plugged himself into his video game. Some of his friends must've been online as well, because I could hear him calling out commands to his troops.

"I got a nuke!" he called out.

Groaning, I managed to leverage myself off my bed. Even as tired as I was, I'd probably sleep better with my door shut. The last thing I wanted was to dream about being on a recon mission, taking out the enemy with sniper shots.

I'd much rather have my dreams filled with Matt. My thoughts were bursting with how perfect my day had been. With my fingers curled around my pendant, I closed my eyes and wished for something good to come of this new friendship.

※ ※ ※

The most glorious week of my life flew by because every day had Matt included in it somehow. Whether it was a simple phone call, or him coming over, we were in constant contact. Thank goodness Hunter liked him; he could have made this so difficult otherwise.

When Matt started telling us about his little brother, I realized I was hearing the same thing my siblings probably felt about me as we were growing up. It made my heart ache all over again for the pain they were going through.

For some reason, I didn't shut down when Jimmy's symptoms were described to me. If this had been talked about during one of the group meetings, I'm sure I would've acted differently. It made me hate how I'd been acting. Those people deserved my same sympathy as I so willingly gave to Matt.

"You know, I just realized the age difference between you and Jimmy is the same as that between myself and Julia. Strange, huh?" I turned my head toward where Matt lay next to me on the front lawn. We tended to have our most serious conversations out here in the sunshine. I think it made Matt feel less hopeless.

"Do you think my brother will get included in a drug trial?"

A gut-wrenching feeling twisted inside me. I didn't want to give him false hope. After hearing that his brother was already using a wheelchair and a feeding tube, I knew he was no longer an ideal candidate. My silence must have lasted too long.

"Chances aren't good, are they?" he asked quietly.

I reached over and intertwined my fingers with his. This was the first time I had purposely touched him. While the idea of it would have thrilled me at any other time, now I only wanted to give him the comfort of my touch.

I couldn't say what I was thinking out loud. I didn't want to be the one to take away his hope for his brother. The tear dripping down the side of my face said more than I ever could. Matt didn't need my sorrow; he needed my strength. I would be there for him through all of this because I'd already walked this painful trail with so many of my Batten afflicted friends over the years.

THE RIFT IN OUR REALITY

๛ ⋙๛⋘

Matt left early on the day my family was set to arrive back home. He decided to make himself scarce, but that only made me like him more. I already missed him, but I was also excited about the family reunion. With everything that had happened with Matt while they were gone, I desperately needed to talk to Julia about it.

Maybe he was afraid of what my parents would think of him hanging around while they weren't here. I guess there might be something to that. Although, Hunter had spent almost every moment with us, so I was never in any danger.

Not that I ever thought I would be, but I'm sure my mom would come to that conclusion straight off. Or maybe that would be Dad's role since Matt's of an age where he could ask me out. Just thinking along those lines made me feel tingly inside, like butterflies fluttering in my stomach.

When I heard the front door opening, I was surprised. Not that they were coming home, but that they were earlier than they normally arrived home. Usually, it would be after dark, but this time it was only mid-afternoon. I left my room to investigate.

The first thing I heard was Julia's happy squeal at seeing me. I knew she'd be rushing over for a hug and braced myself for the impact. Holding out my arms, I grinned in welcome. Once her arms were around me, I said, "I've got so much to talk to you about."

"It's gonna have to wait. We've got the best surprise for you! Come outside. Hurry!"

"Outside? What's going on, Julia?"

Julia grabbed my arm, propelling me through the living room and out the front door. I don't think I've ever seen her this animated. Well, except for the time Ross proposed to her. I couldn't imagine what would get her so enthusiastic, but I was soon to find out.

Something wet pushed itself against my palm. I jerked my hand away, shocked that nobody had warned me. Then I noticed the silence. It was like they were waiting for my reaction. "What's going on?" I asked, but everyone remained silent.

Then I felt the furry body pushing itself against my legs. I heard the panting of a large dog. It hit me all at once. This was the dog I'd been asking for! "Is this what I think it is? Is it a seeing-eye dog?"

I knelt, my hands brushing along the warm fur as I went. Soon enough the dog began licking my neck and cheek. The rush of emotions rendered me speechless, and I felt tears of joy falling down my cheeks.

"Do you like him?" Mom asked, her voice breathless.

"Him? It's a boy? What's his name?"

"Charlie," Dad answered, his voice coming from directly across the dog from me.

"Is Charlie really mine?" I wanted to make sure I was getting this right. If he were only going to be the family dog, then I needed to get my emotions in check.

"He's all yours, baby. We picked him up from a trainer in Northern California. He's been working with Charlie to teach him how to take care of your special needs. Now, he's not a registered service dog, but he will do everything you need."

I didn't need to hear anything beyond that he's mine. I'd done enough research to know why they wouldn't want a registered service dog. Not to mention the fact I'd overheard their hushed conversations on how hard it'd be for the family to have to give him up. If anything were to happen to me, then the dog would get reassigned to another blind person. My parents would want the ability to keep the dog as a reminder of me.

"I already love him." My hands went around the dog as I pulled him closer to me while I hugged him. He was the perfect size. "Tell me about him! I want to know everything you know about him."

Mom took up the storytelling, probably because she knew Dad wouldn't give me enough details to satisfy my every need. "He was surrendered to the trainer from a family who had allergies. They loved him for his first year but had to give him up. Chris, the trainer, has been working with him for many months.

"When we contacted him, we told him what you were like, and he thought he had the perfect plan. I hope you don't mind we sent him your Mr. Octopus so Charlie would recognize your scent. We brought it back with us."

"I wondered what happened to him. Remember, I asked you if you'd seen it. I can't believe you lied to me!" I grinned at my mom's duplicity, yet I really couldn't care less about the loss of my stuffed animal if it meant I could have a real-live one in its place.

"All for a good cause, Haley."

"I'm just teasing you, Mom. I knew you and Julia were up to something. I even asked her about it the night before you all left."

Juila chuckled and said, "And I remember telling you that you're too perceptive for your own good. I so wanted to tell you about Charlie, but we all agreed you should meet him first. If the two of you didn't get along, then we didn't want you to get your hopes up."

I couldn't imagine a dog I wouldn't like. He felt so similar to the dogs we used to have. I hugged him closer to me, thinking about the Labradors we'd had when I was little. They were the best companions, bringing me so much peace during those scary times while I was rapidly losing my sight. I'm sure Charlie's fur was getting quite wet with all the tears I kept producing from sheer joy.

"So, Charlie here," Mom continued, and I could feel her hands caressing Charlie's back as she spoke, "he's trained in walking with someone with vision impairment. He's also been trained to lead you while you ride a bike."

"What? I haven't ridden in years!"

"Well, that's another thing we've been looking into. It seems, there've been studies done with Parkinson's patients who have maintained better mental health if they ride a standard bike."

"So you want me to give it a try? Where? I mean, the road out front isn't really ideal since there aren't any sidewalks."

I couldn't believe Mom was suggesting this. I thought she wanted to keep me safely wrapped up in ribbons here at home. Now she wanted me to ride a bike? What happened to my mom while they were on this trip?

"No, we were thinking of going to a nearby park. At least say you'll give it a try."

"Definitely! I want to do everything with Charlie. At least I won't have to worry about him walking me into any poles. Huh, Dad?" I couldn't help the mischievous dig at my dad.

"Hey, I only did that once. Okay, maybe twice."

"Try three times. That last time, I had a goose egg on my forehead for school pictures."

"That was when you were in the fourth grade. You can't hold that against me forever."

"Nope. Definitely not now that you've made up for it with a properly trained dog. I forgive you, Dad." I kissed Charlie's neck and breathed in his uniquely spicy scent. He certainly didn't smell like our dogs used to.

"You're too kind." Dad chuckled good-naturedly.

"He feels big. What kind of dog is he?" I asked Mom.

"He's a golden lab."

"I knew it!"

Mom continued, "He's going to be two years old on August twenty-third."

"Are you kidding? That's my birthday."

"I know, right? When I heard that, I just knew he was meant to be yours."

I brought my hand up until I found Mom's. I pulled it away from the dog and placed it against my cheek. "Thank you so much, Mom. I know what this means for you, and I appreciate your gesture."

"I know you've wanted more freedom for quite some time. I just had to be sure we found the right companion for you. When I saw Charlie's picture, I just knew he was the one. Now, seeing him with you, we were absolutely right."

"Come on, Haley. Let's show you what Charlie already knows. Your world is about to get so much bigger!" Dad's voice beamed with pride.

"I'm ready to learn!" I stood up, waiting expectantly, not knowing what to do next.

Mom placed Charlie's leash in my hand. She was letting me go. Already I felt different. Today marked the first day of my independence. I was going to be able to go everywhere with Charlie as my guide and protector.

No longer would I have to argue with my parents about not wanting to use a cane. Nobody would look at me like I was a freak if I were just walking with a dog. I could easily pretend I was just like everybody else my age.

I could hardly wait to show him off to Matt. Just thinking about Matt's absence made me realize how much I missed sharing this moment with him. But there was always tomorrow.

Chapter Eight

I knew this was going to be a hard day. How do I convince my best friend, who is also in love with me, that I'm happily starting a relationship with another guy? During the week that Jackson's family was off to Disneyland on vacation, it was easy to push aside the anxiety I knew I'd have when he got back home.

Sure enough, Jackson's first stop was my house. Jackson's initial reaction and introduction to Charlie had been a perfect excuse for me to delay the inevitable. We spent most of the afternoon outside in the sunshine. I kept expecting Matt to walk over, as he usually did, but we remained uninterrupted.

Then came the fun part of Jackson's visit. As usual, he came laden with gifts he'd picked up for me at the theme park. Way to make me feel even guiltier, Jackson!

Usually, I'm thrilled to receive the trinkets because he always picks the coolest gifts. I'm sure he drove all the salespeople crazy because he insisted on feeling, smelling, or hearing everything before he bought it. Jackson's just thoughtful like that; he always wants to bring me a sensory experience beyond what others can see.

Still, I had to tell him the truth as soon as I had a good opening, but I hated the idea of hurting Jackson's feelings. My fingers played with the edges of my necklace as I waited for the right time to bring up Matt.

My nervous gesture must have tipped off Jackson, because he stopped mid-sentence and asked, "What's bothering you, Haley?"

Immediately my hand dropped from the pendant as if I'd been called out by a teacher for talking in class. I'm sure I looked completely guilty, but I tried to play it off cool. Obviously, I'm not very convincing because Jackson wasn't having any of it.

"Don't try to avoid the question, Haley. I know you better than any other person alive. You're hiding something from me. If you don't start talking, then I'm going to take these gifts back home with me right now."

I could feel Jackson picking up the little music box from where it rested on my knee. My hand shot out and captured his wrist, a lucky shot on my part. "I'm sorry, Jackson. I just don't know how to bring it up. I don't want to hurt you."

The silence lingered between us for a few tense seconds. Then Jackson sighed, and I felt his hand release the music box and come to rest on my knee. I dreaded what was going to come next.

"So you're seeing that guy who was talking with you outside the meeting, huh?"

"What? How'd you guess?"

"Well, I could say I'm just that good, but in reality, Hunter already told me about him."

"Seriously?! Why would Hunter tell you about him?"

"Don't worry; he wasn't tattling on you. He just happened to mention something about your new neighbor who also enjoys making videos. He suggested we get together to come up with a new project to work on this summer."

"So, you're not mad at me?"

Jackson coughed lightly as if he were trying to collect himself before answering. "No. I could never be mad at you. Besides, Hunter said he's a really cool guy, and the two of you have fun together. I wouldn't ever want to get in the way of your happiness."

I don't know what I ever did to get such an amazing best friend, but he said all the right things. Before I could control myself, I flung my arms around him and hugged him close. Luckily he was used to my spontaneous gestures of affection, so he just went with it.

Later, I'd think back on this and wonder how much it hurt him to see me so happy with someone other than himself. I couldn't help whom my heart chose to fall for. I'm just thankful I didn't have to choose between my best friend and my budding relationship.

I pulled away, and asked, "Do you want to walk over to his house and meet him?"

"Sure," Jackson answered brightly, maybe a touch too enthusiastically.

I only heard the agreement; I didn't want to hear anything else. In an instant, my excitement returned, pushing my introspective self into the far reaches of my mind. How much better could today get?

My best friend and my...I don't really know what to call him. Well, I'll just go with what my heart dictates. My best friend and my boyfriend were going to become good friends because of me. We were going to have the best summer ever.

As soon as my feet touched the carpet, I felt Charlie push his body against my legs. His training proved impeccable for anticipating my needs. One hand went down to locate his collar while my other found the leash on the nightstand so I could snap the two together. I'm sure that in no time at all, this action would become second nature.

Within seconds, I was standing and ready to head out. "Let's go," I announced brightly, already anticipating and slightly dreading the introductions. This had to go well because I didn't have a plan B.

Having already walked together all over my own yard, it was a simple matter to stick to the driveway until we reached the road. I turned to the left and felt Charlie shift, so he kept his body between me and the road.

I felt a thrill of excitement at the idea of having the freedom to leave without the worry of walking into traffic. Charlie was the perfect companion, his stride keeping in perfect time with my own. After walking a couple of hundred feet, I realized I had no idea how much farther it was to Matt's house.

"Jackson?" I'm sure my voice sounded as concerned as I suddenly felt.

"Yeah?"

"I don't really know how to direct Charlie to go to Matt's house. I've never actually been there. Can you lead the way?"

Jackson chuckled even as he placed my hand on his arm. This was our usual way of walking together, and it suddenly felt right to return to what I'd known for so long. I didn't need to be independent around Jackson; he never made me feel disabled. "I'm glad to know I haven't been rendered completely useless."

"Never, Jackson. I'm always going to need you by my side. We're inseparable, remember?"

"I'm glad you still think so. I was starting to get worried."

My steps faltered, and I pulled Jackson to a stop before we went any farther. "I'm serious, Jackson. I may be starting a relationship with Matt, but that doesn't change what I feel for you. You've always been my best friend, and I don't want anything to change that. Please tell me you agree."

"Definitely, Haley. C'mon, let's get the introductions over. Besides, it's not like I haven't already met him." Jackson resumed walking.

His words came out cheerfully, but I could hear the strain in them. He was only doing this because I had asked it of him. It may have been wishful thinking on my part, but I hoped everything I said about our friendship would always be true.

We turned into Matt's driveway, and I felt Jackson's hesitation. Deciding to try to lighten the mood, I teased, "What's wrong, Jackson? Are you getting cold feet?"

Without responding, Jackson started jogging, forcing me to match his pace or get left alone. He'd never acted like this before, and it started to scare me. As suddenly as he started running, he stopped dead in his tracks. I fully bumped into him and almost fell down.

"Something's not right, Haley. Stay here!"

He forcefully moved my hand off of him and left me standing in the middle of the driveway. I could hear his feet crunching on the loose gravel as he approached the house. Terror filled me as I imagined all sorts of nefarious scenarios which I was actually unable to see. The unknown was killing me. "What's going on, Jackson? Talk to me!"

"Just wait right there, Haley. I mean it. Don't move."

I could feel my limbs start to shake as fear began to overwhelm me. Never in all my imagination could I imagine this meeting going in this direction. There was a reason I didn't watch scary movies, and I certainly didn't want to be participating in something scary in real life. I could hear Jackson calling out from a distance, but it wasn't directed toward me, but the occupants of the house.

Just when I was about to start to really panic, I heard Jackson's heavy breathing and his feet pounding on the gravel coming toward me. At least, I hoped it was him. "Jackson?" I called out.

Relief coursed through me when he spoke.

"Yeah, it's me. Look, Haley, I think something bad must've happened."

"Why?"

"Well, the front door's hanging open. There aren't any cars in the driveway, and I just went through the entire house, and there's nobody home."

"What do you mean, nobody's home? Why was the front door open? Should we call the police?"

"No, I don't think anyone entered the house. It looked more like they all left in a hurry."

"But that doesn't make any sense. Where would they go? Is there stuff still in the house, or did they take everything with them?" I could feel a lead weight on my heart. Could it be possible the Dietrich family decided to move away? Why wouldn't Matt have told me? Was he gone from my life before I even got the chance to say goodbye?

"No, their stuff was all still there. Do you have your phone? Maybe we should call the authorities?" Jackson's hand touched my shoulder, his familiarity already starting to calm me from my worst fears, even though I was still worried.

I dug in my pants pocket and pulled out my phone. Handing it over to him, I realized I should have heard from Matt before now. How come I hadn't thought to call him? I know I'd been preoccupied with training Charlie, but that was hardly a good excuse to ignore our budding relationship.

"Good grief, Haley. You've got six missed calls and dozens of text messages from Matt. Why didn't you answer him?"

"I do? I never heard anything. What did he say?"

"Oh, here's the problem. Your ringer was turned off, and you don't have the notifications turned on for your texts. I swear, Haley, I go away for a week, and you messed everything up."

"I don't care about that right now, Jackson. What did Matt say?" I know Jackson was deflecting from the real problem, but I was too concerned for Matt to play along.

Jackson groaned and said, "His little brother's in serious condition. They took him to the hospital, and he's asked you to come to be with him. Well, I guess that explains why the door was left open."

"Call him right now, Jackson. I've got to tell him I wasn't ignoring him. I can't believe I didn't check to make sure the ringer was turned on. I'm such an idiot!"

"C'mon, let's head back to your house. I'll call him when we get back to my truck. We can head straight to the hospital."

"Thanks, Jackson. You're the best!"

ಌ ೧ೀ೦ ೧

Sitting in the truck with Charlie between my feet on the floor, I held the ringing phone up to my ear. I desperately hoped Matt wasn't furious with me for ignoring him. At least, that's what he would have thought I was doing until I had a chance to explain what happened.

The call was picked up, and I almost yelled in anticipation of what I was certain to hear. "Matt? Are you there?"

"Yeah, Haley, it's me."

I felt terrible when I heard his dejected-sounding tone. "Matt, I just found out about your calls and messages. My ringer was off and...oh, never mind. How's Jimmy? We're on our way to meet you right now."

Matt's voice broke, and I could hear him trying to hold back his crying. With a valiant effort, he managed to say, "It's bad, Haley. The doctors don't think he's going to make it. I feel so useless."

"I'm so sorry, Matt. We'll be there before you know it. Where are you exactly?"

"He's in the ICU. I'll meet you outside. I'll head out there right now."

As per his usual, he abruptly hung up the phone. I should have been used to it by now, but I still found it disconcerting. Maybe it was his emotional state which caused him to be more abrupt than usual; I'd probably be the same way.

Bringing the phone down to rest in my lap, my other hand clutched my pendant as I prayed. I knew it was vain to hope; based on Matt's descriptions of his brother's symptoms, Jimmy's disease was more advanced than any of them knew or wanted to admit. I'd seen it all before with other Batten friends. My best hope would be for Jimmy to have an easy and swift passing.

"Hurry, Jackson; Matt sounded so scared. Jimmy's not doing well."

My heart went out to the Dietrich family. They were entering another phase of their lives which they all wanted to keep at bay forever. I almost felt guilty since my disease had taken a different path with the first round of trial drugs. Otherwise, my family would've already gone through the grief they were facing right now.

"Yeah, I kinda gathered as much. I'm going as fast as I dare. It'll only be a couple more minutes. I'll drop you off out front and go find a parking space."

"Thanks, Jackson. Matt said he'd wait for me outside the ICU." I wished I didn't know the layout of the hospital so well to know already where Matt would be. I'd spent too much time there, more time than any teenager should have any right.

Chapter Nine

"Hey, I see a spot in short-term parking," Jackson announced as he turned into the spot. "I don't see Matt anywhere. I'll just walk in with you."

As soon as I opened the passenger door, Charlie jumped down onto the ground and stood waiting for me to get out. With his leash in my left hand, my right hand automatically reached for Jackson. As usual, he took his place to lead me to the entrance. I didn't like the idea that Matt wasn't outside. I had a terrible feeling in my gut.

The doors slid open allowing the antiseptic air to blow into my face. I hated that smell. Before we took more than three steps into the lobby, a woman's voice called out.

"Miss. Miss! You're not allowed to bring pets into the hospital," she announced rudely.

I shook my head in denial and retorted, "He's a seeing-eye dog; he's not a pet."

"I'm sorry, Miss. But without the proper documentation, you won't be able to stay here with your dog. It's hospital policy."

With this being my first outing, I was at a loss for what to do or say. Luckily, Jackson stepped in and saved me.

"I'll just take him back to the truck. Call me when you're ready to go home."

I had to temper my anger at the hospital representative because I didn't want to jeopardize my ability to stay here for Matt. Still, to be denied access to the hospital simply because of a technicality seemed so wrong. I reluctantly handed over the leash to Jackson.

"Thank you," I said to him.

"Hey, no problem. Charlie probably has to go to the bathroom anyway."

Knowing Jackson the way I did, he would probably find the employees car and encourage Charlie to pee on her tires. Now I was left alone in the lobby with only the company of the receptionist. I hated to ask her anything, but I also didn't want to be hanging around awkwardly in the middle of the room. "I'm expecting to meet someone. Can you take me to a seat to wait?"

"Sure, they're right over here."

The woman's voice moved, but with all the other noises in the room, I lost track of where she had gone. Turning, I attempted to follow her only to bump into someone. "I'm sorry," I instantly apologized before I recognized Matt's cologne. "Matt? Is that you?"

"Yes, I'm so glad you're here." His arms crushed me to his chest. If the situation hadn't been so dire, then I might have enjoyed the contact. Instead, I wrapped my arms around his middle and let him draw support from me.

A minute passed in silence while he collected himself. "Why're you here alone? Where's Hunter?"

"Never mind that. Let's go sit down so you can tell me about Jimmy. What's going on?" A fresh wave of grief washed over Matt, and I didn't know where to take him. If only the receptionist hadn't abandoned me in the lobby, then maybe this scene could have been avoided.

Matt's hand grabbed onto mine, and I could feel him trembling with emotion. We walked several feet before Matt directed me to sit in one of the plush visitor's chairs. He kept my hand in his as he seated himself next to me.

The silence grew between us, but I could hear him sniffling as his emotions kept him from speaking. I finally asked, "Tell me what happened, Matt."

With a loud inhalation through his nose, Matt spoke haltingly. "We thought Jimmy was sleeping. He's been so tired lately."

"When was this?"

"Two days ago."

My mind reeled. That was the day my parents brought Charlie home to me. All this time, Matt needed me, and I was oblivious to it all. When Matt continued his story, I simply listened.

"Mom went to check on him and started screaming. I ran into the room and saw Jimmy's face was almost blue. I shoved Mom out of the way and dragged Jimmy off the bed and onto the floor. I started doing CPR immediately and begged him to be okay.

"We weren't thinking clearly. Mom and I rushed him out to the car where she drove, and I kept trying to resuscitate him. She called the hospital to let them know we were on the way.

"As soon as we pulled up to the emergency exit, the nurses took him from us. Mom called Dad, and he rushed over to be with us, but we still hadn't heard anything yet about his condition. I assumed that meant it was good news.

"About an hour later, a doctor came out to talk with us. He said that Jimmy had a seizure which caused him to stop breathing. They put him on life-support, but they didn't hold out too much hope for his recovery. He said there's no way of telling how long Jimmy had been without oxygen."

"Oh, Matt; I'm so sorry." I clutched his hand in between both of mine. There was nothing I could say or do which would make this any easier, but I hoped I could bring him some comfort. "So, there hasn't been any change? That's good, right?"

I could feel Matt's body start to shake as his emotions once again began to take over his self-control. Not knowing what else to do, I dropped my knees onto the floor in front of him and pulled my hands away from his so I could put them around his middle.

I don't know how long we stayed that way, and I didn't care what people might think about our display of emotion. Matt needed this physical contact; I could tell by the way his hands held me so tightly.

"He's gone, Haley." A fresh wave of grief came over him, rendering him speechless again.

I shook my head, wanting to deny the truth I already knew even before entering the hospital. "No, don't say that, Matt. He might come out of this yet."

"No. That was the reason I wasn't out here when you came in. The doctors all agreed that he was brain dead.

They asked my parents for permission to turn off his life-support. I couldn't hang around and watch them turn off the machines, Haley. I ran away. I failed my little brother."

"No, Matt. You didn't fail him. You did everything you could to keep him alive until you got here. Nobody would ever fault you for what you did for him."

"But I could feel his life slipping away from me. Every time I breathed into him, it felt less like the boy I knew and more like some stranger. How terrible is that for me to say? I'm the worst brother ever."

"No, Matt, no. Don't say that. Jimmy loved you. It was his time to go. Nothing anyone could have done would have brought him back. He's at peace now, Matt. He's not in any more pain."

"No, because he's dead. I'll never get to see him smile at me again. How can I keep going on knowing he's not a part of my life anymore?"

"That's where you're wrong, Matt. Jimmy will always be a part of you." I pulled my face away from his chest and put my hand over his heart. "Right here, you keep all your memories of Jimmy. He'll always be with you."

"It's not enough, Haley. He deserved so much more." Matt couldn't keep talking as his crying prevented him from continuing.

§ⓒ෩ⓒ℞

I'm not sure how much time passed, but my knees were killing me. Nothing could have forced me to move, though, not when Matt held me so desperately. Two people appeared at once behind me.

"There you are, Matt. I've been looking everywhere for you," a man spoke.

"Haley," Hunter spoke my name.

Matt and I sprang apart as though we'd been caught doing something wrong. I attempted to stand up, but both of my feet were asleep. My brother's arm supported me as I stumbled awkwardly. "Where's Jackson?"

"He came home an hour ago."

"Hey, Dad. Is it over?" Matt asked.

I could tell he had stood up from the sound of his voice. Never before had I wanted someone to deny what Matt was asking. I dreaded the answer along with him.

"Yes. He's very peaceful now. Your mom wants you to say your goodbyes to him. She wants us to say a prayer with him as a family."

"Sure. Um, I'll see you later, Haley."

Hunter slung his arm across my shoulders, his hand squeezing my arm as he knew how this news would affect me. He had seen this scene too many times himself. It never got any easier.

"Let's go home," Hunter said quietly, respecting the sanctity of the moment.

I nodded, unable to speak because I bit my lip so hard to keep from losing it here in public. I let him lead me out of the hospital and into the fresh air and warm sunshine which seemed so at odds to how cold I felt inside. The world was a little darker because yet another child had been lost to Batten disease.

As soon as I stepped into my house, Charlie pushed up against me, whining and pawing at me in a way he had never done before. I'm sure he could feel my sorrow, and it helped tremendously to hug his warm body close to me while my tears overflowed my eyes and dropped into his fur. I felt empty inside, like Jimmy's death was the last one I could endure.

I couldn't be around anyone right now. Silently standing up, I walked away from my family to hide out in my bedroom. When I curled up on my bed, Charlie jumped up and stretched out next to me, his muzzle resting on my forearm while his whining seemed to mirror my sorrow.

ಸಂಜಾತಿ

The ringing of my phone in my pants pocket roused me from my dreams. I didn't remember falling asleep, but the instant I woke, my only thought was for Matt. If that were him calling, I needed to answer it. He needed me more now than ever.

I rolled over onto my back, surprised to find Charlie still snuggled next to me. By the third ring, I had the phone in my hand. Bringing it up to my ear, I wondered what time it was.

"Hey, Haley," Matt spoke, his voice soft and gentle. "Did I wake you?"

I ran my hand over my face, feeling the dried tears on my cheeks. "Yes, but that's okay. I probably shouldn't be sleeping anyway. What time is it?"

"Six-thirty."

"Yeah, I definitely should get up to have dinner. My mom hates it when I miss meals."

"You already missed it, Haley. It's six-thirty in the morning."

"Oh, well, that's unexpected." I blew a breath out of my lips as I processed Matt's news. I tried to shove Charlie over to give me room to move, but he stubbornly remained where he was. "Move, you big brute," I spoke to him.

"Who's with you?" Matt asked, his voice not nearly as gentle as it had been.

"My dog. I can't get him to move out of my way."

"When did you get a dog?"

"My parents surprised me with him when they got back from their trip. We were bringing him over to your house when we found out..." I stopped as soon as I realized where I was leading this conversation. Matt didn't need a reminder of yesterday; I'm sure it was fresh on his mind.

"Yeah. Well. Can I see you today?"

"Sure. When do want to come over?"

"Um. How about now? I mean, I know it's early, but I need to talk to you."

"Absolutely. You don't need to explain it to me. Just head on over, and I'll meet you outside. Give me about five minutes to wash up first, okay?"

Already, my heart raced in anticipation of being with him again. Was it terrible that I just wanted to be near him? I know he was hurting really badly because of his brother, but I was so happy I was the one he wanted to seek comfort from.

"Great. I'll see you in six minutes."

I had to chuckle at Matt's abrupt end to the call. I set the phone down on my nightstand and managed to climb over the dog. I knew he was awake; I just didn't know why he refused to move.

I hauled off my wrinkled clothes and grabbed the first things which came to my hands. It didn't really matter what they were, but I was thankful they were thicker material. The mornings were still slightly chilly, and I had no idea how long Matt and I would be sitting outside.

After freshening up in the bathroom, I returned to my room only to discover Charlie had moved from the bed to sit in front of my dresser. I stubbed my toe on him, but he managed to stand up to give me leverage to keep from falling over.

"At least you're slightly helpful," I muttered as I reached over him to grab my phone and his leash. Together, we left my room and entered a totally quiet living room. This wasn't my usual time to be up, mostly because I liked my sleep. But it was odd to have everything so still around the house.

I felt myself relaxing as soon as I opened the front door and heard the first birds beginning to start chirping. At least nature was still going on like normal, even if nothing else remained the same. Charlie tugged urgently on the leash in my hand, something he'd never done before.

Quickly pulling the door shut behind me, I let Charlie take the lead he obviously wanted. I just hoped he wasn't planning on chasing a squirrel or something stupid like that. When Charlie began barking, I worried he would wake up my parents. "Shush, Charlie. That's enough!" I spoke sternly.

Abruptly Charlie stopped, and I heard him whimpering and licking someone. "Who's this, Haley?"

"Matt, I didn't know you were there. This's my dog, Charlie."

"Charlie? That's so strange. He looks just like my old dog who was also named Charlie. Don't you, boy? Who's a good boy?"

I could only assume Matt was rubbing Charlie as he spoke nonsense to him. I knelt next to the pair of them, my hand resting on Charlie's back. "I didn't know you used to have a dog. Tell me about him."

"Oh, we got him when he was a puppy. He was the cutest little guy, so friendly, just like this fellow. Anyway, we discovered that Jimmy..." he choked up a bit but managed to continue after he cleared his throat. "We found out Jimmy was allergic to dogs and we had to give him up."

I felt something stirring inside me. Could this be possible? I had to find out. "How old was Charlie when you gave him up?"

"Just over a year. Why?"

"Who did you give him to?"

"A friend of the family. He's a great dog trainer and said he'd find him a good home."

"Oh my gosh! Matt! I think this is your Charlie. My parents got him from a trainer named Chris in Northern California."

"No way! Are you serious? Charlie, is it you, buddy?"

As much as I wanted the independence that Charlie would give me, I knew I couldn't keep the dog. Matt needed his canine companion back, especially now. "You have to take him back, Matt. I can't keep him knowing he was yours first."

"What? No, Haley. He was trained for you. I'm glad he has a purpose. Besides, it'll give me an excuse to come and see you more often."

I wasn't sure if I should be thrilled or offended. Did he just admit he would be coming around to see the dog instead of me? The more logical part of my brain decided I liked any reason for Matt to spend time with me even if it were just for Charlie.

Chapter Ten

Two days later, I stood beside Matt at Jimmy's memorial service, with Charlie standing at attention between us. I wore my lavender dress which I saved for these somber occasions. I'm sure it received some looks of disapproval from the guests, but they needed to be reminded of the good times and not focus solely on the sorrow they felt right now.

Charlie and I both served as Matt's support crew. Although, I have a feeling Charlie brought Matt more comfort. They shared memories with Jimmy which I didn't have.

When the service ended, Matt offered to drive me home and spend the afternoon with me. I gladly accepted. He needed a distraction from his distraught parents.

Matt pulled into my driveway and sighed. "It looks like you've got company. Maybe I should go."

"What kind of car is it?"

"A Ford truck."

"Oh, that's just Jackson. C'mon, it's time the two of you

got to know one another."

"I don't know. The last time we met, he didn't seem that thrilled with me."

"That's only because he doesn't know you. I promise he'll be on his best behavior. Get out of the car; you're coming inside." I opened my door and got out, Charlie happily leading the way.

"Yes, ma'am," Matt said, just before I shut the door.

I heard his car door shut and grinned at how easily he followed my direction. I hated it when boys tried to be difficult. I'd had plenty of practice with Hunter, so he was no match for my determination. Besides, I needed Matt and Jackson to become friends if I were going to have the summer of my dreams.

The room fell silent as soon as we walked in. They must have been evaluating how Matt's mood would be considering where we'd just come from. I could have kissed Jackson for coming to the rescue.

"Hey, I'm Jackson. It's good to see you again, Matt."

"Hi, Jackson."

I could only assume they were either shaking hands or staring one another down. Probably both, knowing how boys were with one another.

Jackson suddenly said, "So Hunter was telling me you liked making YouTube videos. We should plan something to work on this summer. What do you think?"

"I'm in!" Matt agreed, his voice more animated than I'd heard it in quite some time.

I should have known Jackson would be amazing. There was a reason he was my best friend. I stood there with a foolish grin on my face until Charlie jiggled the leash in my hand as he sat down beside my feet.

"Did Mom tell you the news, Haley?" Hunter asked suddenly.

I hadn't even realized he was in the room. I frowned slightly, trying to think of anything I was expecting to hear about. I shook my head and said, "I don't think so. What is it?"

"The research study in New York called. They've agreed to allow you into the trial."

"Hey, Hunter! I was going to tell her!" Mom scolded as she walked into the room. Her voice turned toward me as she said, "Isn't that the most wonderful news ever? This's what we've been working for, ever since we got your diagnosis."

My heart thudded dangerously fast. What was this going to mean for me? Was I going to be cured, or was it just going to be another patch to extend my life? I didn't want to get my hopes up until I knew more about it. "When is it?"

"They're getting final approvals right now from the FDA. They think everything will be in place within eight weeks. Aren't you excited?" Mom's hands circled my upper arms, and she squeezed tightly in her happiness at the news.

"Excuse me," I said, suddenly feeling slightly queasy. I pulled away, dropping Charlie's leash and making a mad dash for the sanctuary of my bedroom.

"Haley!" Mom called after me.

My mind reeled with the possibilities ahead of me. Did I want to go through with this? Was it right to go right when Matt lost his brother to the same disease? Did I owe it to

Matt to turn it down? I curled up on my bed, Mr. Octopus held tightly to my chest much like I'd done when I was contemplating my first treatment.

"Haley?" Matt spoke softly from across my room.

"I'm sorry, Matt." I felt tears start to drop from my eyes.

"Sorry? Why, Haley? This is fantastic news."

His voice sounded closer. Just the fact that he was trying to cheer me up only made this worse. How could I explain how I felt about this to him?

"Don't you get it?"

"Get what? That you have a second chance?"

The bed tilted as Matt sat down on the edge. His hand came to rest on my knee, but he didn't attempt to comfort me any further. His kindness only made me cry harder.

"Haley, what's got you so upset? Shouldn't you be happy about this? Explain this to me."

It took me a few seconds to compose myself. When I finally felt I had sufficient control of myself, I said, "It's not right that I'm going to get a second chance when your brother didn't even get a first chance. It's not fair.

"They should be offering this trial to someone younger and in more danger of dying. I can't stand to see another family torn apart because of this awful disease. It's not fair. If I refuse, maybe they'll pick someone who needs it more."

I knew I was rambling and repeating myself, but the words just spilled out of my mouth. I hated even bringing up Jimmy's death to Matt. He needed something to take his mind away from it, not having me throw it in his face.

Matt scooted up until he leaned against the headboard next to me. He slung his arm over my shoulder and shifted my weight over until I rested against his side. If I hadn't been so upset, I would have enjoyed the experience.

"I seem to recall some very knowledgeable girl explaining the trials process to me only last week. She told me that the candidates have to meet certain criteria in order to be accepted. I'm sure if there were better candidates, then they wouldn't have been offering the slot to you.

"Haley, I don't want you to give up this opportunity out of some misguided notion that it'd upset me. In fact, I'm hoping I'll be able to go with you. Would you like that?"

I tipped my face up toward his, and asked, "Are you serious?"

"Definitely. I'd be honored to go with you."

"But it's in New York. How would that work?"

"I've got money saved up. Don't worry about it. If you want me there, then I'll be right by your side. Just tell me that you'll go."

I was happy enough to kiss him right there, but I managed to hold myself back just in time. "Yes. Matt, I'll go if you come with me. Are you sure you're okay with this? I mean...Jimmy?"

"He would've been the first one to want you to go. Trust me."

I flung my arm across his middle and hugged him tightly to me. This was the happiest I'd been in a long time. With my face smashed against Matt's chest, I said, "Thank you."

"Ahem! Am I interrupting something?" Jackson asked rudely from the doorway.

I grinned, imagining the look on Jackson's face. He never seemed to grow up from the six-year-old I could clearly remember. Lifting my head, I said brightly, "Not at all. We need to go tell Mom that we're going to New York."

☙ ❦ ❧

I don't know why it didn't occur to me before, but just by agreeing to participate in the upcoming drug trial, it also meant spending many days at the doctor's office or the hospital to undergo innumerable tests. With only eight weeks to gather as much baseline data as they could, I hated seeing my summer days slip away.

Yet, these days also proved to be quite rewarding. After Matt heard about Charlie being turned away from the hospital, he became furious and vowed to do something about it. I didn't think much of it until one afternoon, about a week later, Matt came over sounding quite pleased with himself.

"What's up with you today?" I asked him as we walked through the yard.

"I've got something for you," he answered, suddenly thrusting a package into my hands.

I felt the padded envelope, not having any idea what it could be. Being visually impaired, I generally didn't handle much mail, so he had me quite curious. "What is it?"

"Why don't you open it and see?" he answered.

"Ha. Ha." I answered, giving him some grief for the phrase he chose to use.

"I'm so sorry, Haley; it just slipped out."

"I'm just teasing, Matt. Don't worry about it. I've long since gotten over being sensitive to it." Although, I realized my family never used any sighted phrases like it anymore.

Just another small consideration they all made on my behalf without my ever having to say anything.

I felt for the edge where the flap folded over. With a bit of tugging, I managed to shred open the top and shove my hand inside. I felt some paperwork, which Matt would have to read to me, but I also felt something made of a thick, embroidered fabric. More than a little confused, I brought it out and asked, "What is it?"

"I contacted Chris, you know, Charlie's trainer. I told him what happened at the hospital and he was as upset as I was. I don't know what he did, but he pulled some strings and made some phone calls. What you're holding in your hand is the certification needed for Charlie to remain with you no matter where you go."

"You mean, this is Charlie's? What does it say?"

"Yes, it attaches to your guide handle, and it reads 'Service Dog.' Now, nobody can turn you away from where you need to go."

Immediately, I felt a sense of unrestrained pleasure at Matt's wonderful gift. No longer would I have to endure hours of alone-time while waiting for my tests and procedures. Charlie could legally be by my side everywhere.

I threw my arms around Matt's neck and automatically planted a kiss on his lips. As soon as we came into contact with one another, I felt the electricity pulsing through me as well as my profound embarrassment at acting so impulsively.

Immediately, I jumped away from him, my fingers reaching up to touch my lips. "I'm so sorry; I just...I'm so sorry." I would have turned to run away, except Matt's hand grabbed my arm and prevented me from bolting.

"I'm not sorry, Haley. I've wanted to do that for a long time."

He let go of my arm, and I stood stupidly staring blankly as my mind processed his confession. "You did?" I whispered, not trusting that I'd heard him correctly.

"Yes. And maybe we'll try it again sometime if you like."

I'm sure the blush overcoming my cheeks must have been quite the sight, but I simply nodded. There was no way I was going to admit that I'd take that sometime right now. Obviously, if he wanted to do it again, he would have. Now, I would just have to wait him out and see if he truly meant what he said, or if he only were trying to make me feel less awkward. I nodded woodenly.

"Let's go put Charlie's new badge of honor on. What do you say?" Matt offered brightly as I continued to stay silent.

ಸಿ ಆ ಲ

Luckily, the boys in my life conspired together to fill my non-doctor days with fun activities. Jackson had proposed we begin doing a video sequence honoring Jimmy. At first, I'd been reluctant to agree, thinking how sad it would make Matt. But, being Jackson, he merely forged ahead and talked to Matt behind my back.

The next thing I knew, we were planning all sorts of activities which Matt had promised his little brother they would do someday when he wasn't sick. I wasn't about to tell any of them that some of these events were also on my bucket list.

With all of this going on, I found myself dropping into my bed every night, more exhausted than I'd ever felt. Yet each morning, I looked forward to whatever the boys had planned for us. This was the first time I truly felt alive and normal. I was living my dreams with the people who made me feel equal to them.

CHAPTER ELEVEN

We were getting ready to leave the house for another epic adventure to be posted on Jackson's YouTube channel. Already, he was getting more motivated because his number of followers had almost tripled just because we'd changed the focus of the videos he was producing. Apparently, people were more interested in action and adventure, than in home movie productions.

What's today's planned activity, you ask? Zip-lining. I'd heard it felt a lot like flying, but I wasn't sure how I felt about it. While it was on my personal bucket list, some things were better to keep as a dream rather than to actually do. But I'd said yes, so I guess I was going no matter how nervous it made me feel.

I'd already changed my outfit three times and ended up choosing my yoga pants and a long-sleeved shirt. Since the weather was warm and sunny, I didn't need to worry about any type of jacket. I pulled my hair into a ponytail low enough to accommodate wearing a helmet.

When we all piled into Matt's car, the excitement was palpable. None of us had ever done this before, and Hunter was especially eager to try out his new head-mounted camera dad had given him the night before. When the boys started talking about some video game they'd discovered recently, I closed my eyes and rested my head against the window. The warmth of Charlie's fur on my side began to lull me to sleep.

Because I'd had trouble sleeping the night before in anticipation of today, I promptly fell asleep and missed the entire drive. I was totally fine with that; it gave me less time to get worked up about it.

This was such a novel feeling for me since I'd always looked forward to daring adventures in my past. Maybe I was finally starting to get common sense or a sense of mortality. In either event, I suppressed the worry and concentrated on enjoying myself to the fullest.

Matt shook me awake before letting himself out of the car. It took me a minute to recall where I was and almost fell out the door when Matt opened it up for me. He gallantly caught me, his hand supporting my elbow as I stood up. I didn't mind the contact.

Rather than letting go, his hand slid down my arm until his fingers curled around mine. This was the first time he'd shown any display of affection with me while Jackson and Hunter were around. Maybe my spontaneous kiss had stirred up something in him, and I was more than happy to explore where this would go.

I don't know if Matt could tell I was nervous and was merely providing a distraction for me, but I loved him even more for it. We walked in front of the others, and I'm pretty sure they were already filming. They liked to get the entire experience documented. The thought flittered through my mind about what my parents would think about Matt holding my hand.

Our guide instructed us on how to wear our harnesses. Again, Matt caught me off-guard when he assisted me into my gear without asking my permission. Just when I thought the day couldn't get any better, the guide told us they had a two-person option.

"I'd like to go with Haley," Matt offered even before I could make the same request.

I bit my bottom lip as I tried to keep the grin from my face. Matt's fingers squeezed mine playfully as if he already knew what I was thinking. He leaned in until his lips tickled my ear and said, "I can't wait to fly with you. I want to watch your face light up with joy."

Like a typical giddy school-girl I used to make fun of with the boys, I giggled. "I can't wait," I stupidly answered. I don't even remember how we got to the platform, but I could feel the breeze on my cheeks as the guide clipped our harnesses onto the overhead wire.

Matt and I were closer than we'd ever been before, except for the time when he comforted me while I was crying. I didn't care what came next, as long as I could have Matt with me.

"Are you ready?" Matt asked, his arm linked with mine.

"Absolutely!" I replied instantly, the thrill of flying right before me. This was the moment I'd dreamed of, but better than I could've planned before meeting Matt.

"One, two, three!" Matt called out before he stepped off the platform and forced me to do the same.

The air whooshed past us; our speed kept increasing as the sound of our harness on the overhead wire kept whirring. My hand clutched Matt's, and I grinned until my cheeks hurt. I was flying!

Faster than I would have thought possible, I felt Matt moving his arm up to start slowing us down. "Already?" I asked.

"Yep. But this is only the first run. We still have five more to go. Do you want to provide the braking on the next one?"

"I don't know. Maybe," I replied, still trying to process how I'd manage it.

A pair of hands came out of nowhere and grabbed my harness to pull me forward onto the platform. I could tell immediately that it wasn't Matt; it definitely wasn't as gentle as I'd known him to be with me. In a few minutes, Hunter and then Jackson joined us on the platform. As a group, we moved on to the next run.

After the last zip-line, the guide asked us to go down the ladder since the small platform was too small for our entire group. He went down first, and I followed him right away. In an instant, Matt and I found ourselves alone in the woods.

As I stepped away from the last rung of the ladder, I stumbled on the uneven ground, and my hands went out to find something to steady me. Immediately, my hands rested on Matt's muscular chest as he caught me up against him.

"Thanks," I said, inhaling his masculine scent, and tipping my head up to grin at him.

He must have seen something in my expression because he decided this was the moment for which he'd been waiting. His lips touched onto mine, gently at first, and then more urgently as I instantly responded to him.

Time seemed to stand still as I melted against him. How could he be so perfect? He made me feel safe and loved. Before we could get too caught up in our own little world, Matt pulled away and whispered, "That's what I've wanted to do since I met you."

"It was worth the wait," I whispered back, my mind racing with giddy thoughts about our future together.

Overhead, I could hear Hunter yelling out to Jackson who was the last to ride on the zip-line. Before we could get razzed by the boys, I stepped away from Matt so there would be some space between us by the time they joined us. Although, Matt didn't let me get too far when he took my hand in his.

"I wouldn't want you to trip," he added.

I could hear the humor in his voice. To be truthful, I was glad for his assistance. I felt slightly at a loss since we'd had to leave Charlie in the main office since they didn't have harnesses for service pets, nor did I think he would enjoy it as much as we did.

ಐ ೞಐ ಚ

I took another nap in the car after the zip-lining adventure. Since this was only our first activity planned for the day, I knew it would be important to get whatever rest I could. Our next stop was a short trail hike to visit some waterfalls.

When we parked the car forty-five minutes later, I felt rested and refreshed. I waited for another five minutes on the park bench while Hunter and Jackson fiddled with their recording equipment. Another car pulled into the parking lot, coming to a stop right beside where I sat.

As soon as I heard the voices, I jumped to my feet, scaring Charlie at my abruptness. "Jay! JB! What're you doing here?" I hadn't spoken with either of these two since our last day of school. This was such a nice surprise.

JB was the first to hug me. His laughter rumbled all through his chest as I held him tightly to me. "Hunter thought you'd be surprised."

"My brother planned this? Thanks, Hunter," I called around JB's body to where I'd last heard my brother laughing with Matt. "I swear you've gotten taller!" I teased.

Jay touched my arm to let me know she was near. She wasn't the type of person who enjoyed physical contact, but she made that exception for my blindness. "We've been watching your videos on YouTube. I'm so glad you've been getting out this summer. I just hope you're not overdoing it."

I shook my head and sighed as I replied, "You sound just like my mother. I'm fine; I promise." I tugged on Charlie's leash to bring him up next to me. I knelt and put my arm over his back, rubbing his chest as I said, "You two need to meet Charlie. He used to be Matt's dog, but through some strange twist of fate, he came to be my seeing-eye dog."

After the pleasant reunion and introductions were made, we began our trek up the first trail. None of them thought this would be something I'd want to do, since seeing nature was the biggest draw to this location. "I just love all the fresh, earthy smells here," I commented.

"Is that why you wanted to come? I mean, tripping on tree roots and rocks hasn't usually been your thing," Hunter teased.

"Very funny." I tried to make a stern face but ended up laughing at him. "You know how much I enjoy being around water. I love the sound of it as it rushes over rocks and falls freely. Plus, there's nothing quite like the mist as it falls all around, sprinkling us with its magical healing powers."

"I don't know about all of that," JB added, "but this sure beats working at the fast-food joint for the day."

We laughed at JB's joke, but then all fell silent as we arrived at the first waterfall. It was everything I had hoped it would be. The volume of water created such a crashing sound as it spilled over the top to land into several pools on its way to the bottom.

Of course, the boys discovered the trail led behind the fall of water. We made the slippery, dangerous journey without too much trouble. The thunder of the fall made conversations all but impossible until we came away from it on the other side.

Matt lifted my hand to his lips, planting a kiss on my knuckles. "Did you like that?"

"Yes. It was exhilarating."

"Are you sure? You actually look pretty beat. Do you want to head back to the car? We can wait there while the others finish the trail. Hunter thinks it'll take them about an hour to make the circuit."

"Okay, maybe we should go back." Plus I liked the idea of being alone with Matt. I'd never been parked with a boy before and wondered if it were everything everyone made it out to be. Maybe I'd get an opportunity to find out.

"Hey, guys. We're heading back to the car. See you when you're done," Matt called out to the group which had moved on ahead of us.

"Are you sure? We could all go now," Jackson offered.

"No. Go finish your video tour. I'll be fine," I answered, probably a bit too quickly to be entirely convincing. From the catcalls and whistles which immediately followed, I must have been too obvious. I'm sure Jackson captured my flaming red cheeks on camera, yet I couldn't bring myself to care overly much.

Back at the car, Matt and I scooted into the back seat together. Charlie had made himself at home across the front seat, leaving us room to get cozy. Matt leaned against the door, and I rested my back against Matt. He had his arms around my middle, and I traced the outlines of his hands where they splayed across my stomach.

"What're you thinking about? I can almost feel the wheels turning in your head," Matt teased.

I loved how his breath tickled the edges of my ear. It brought shivers of anticipation immediately. This day would be forever cemented into my memory as the perfect summer day. Then I had to go and ruin it with my curiosity.

"What're your plans for your future?" I asked.

"Don't you mean our future?" Matt turned his hand over and captured mine with his. "I've never known how lonely I was until I met you. I wake up thinking about you, I spend all day with you, and I fall asleep with you on my mind."

"I'm surprised you don't dream about me as well," I said, laughing at his sudden seriousness.

"Oh, but I do. Those are the best. Do you want me to tell

you about them?"

"Not just now. I'm serious, Matt. What're your plans? I mean, I'm sure you want to go off to college, have a career, a family." I bit my lip, holding back the rush of emotions I felt as I thought about his future without me in it.

"I do. With you, Haley. We've got a lifetime to plan. Once you're done with your treatment, you'll see how much better you'll feel."

"What do you know about it?"

"I know that it's had some pretty spectacular results so far. There's no reason in the world to think it won't be the same for you as well."

"Those were all in the lab rats. We can't be sure of anything just yet."

"Well, I'll believe in it until you do as well. You'll see. Once it's all said and done, we can celebrate the fact that I was right."

"Oh, you'd like that, wouldn't you?" I pushed my elbow back into his gut.

"Being right? Absolutely!" Matt didn't get to hear my response. He shifted me over slightly and brought his lips down to cover mine.

I forgot all of my misgivings and objections in an instant. Who needed to worry about the future when the present was so pleasurable? I could live in this moment forever.

Chapter Twelve

Six days before we were scheduled to leave for New York, I woke up with a stuffy nose. Who ever heard of someone catching a cold in the middle of summer? I was just grateful everyone was too busy to notice my sniffling.

I didn't dare ask anyone to give me any medicine to relieve the stuffiness. I could just imagine the uproar any bout of a minor illness would create at this late date. At least almost all of my family had plans for the morning.

At ten o'clock, Hunter knocked on my open bedroom door just to get my attention. "Everyone's gone, and I've set up your cello in the living room. Are you ready?"

"Sure," I answered, forcing myself to have the energy to get up.

"Are you okay?"

"Yeah; I just didn't sleep that great last night."

For the next hour, I played through several of the songs I'd been writing while Hunter filmed and directed me to start over at various points. For once, I wished I could simply play straight through and be done already. But since I'd asked for Hunter's help, I had to keep my snarky comments to myself.

When he finally declared he had everything he needed, I sighed with relief. My arm felt like a noodle, and my hand was cramping from holding the bow for so long. At least I'd managed to play well despite being so tired.

I returned my bow to its special case and thought seriously about taking another nap. Just as I turned to sit down on my bed, Hunter stopped at my doorway.

"I'm heading out for a few hours. Are you going to be okay alone?"

"Yes." I couldn't withhold the irritation from my voice. "It's not like I'm six, Hunter. Besides, I've got Charlie to look out for me. Go and have fun. I think I'll just take a nap anyway."

"Cool. See you later. Cooper and I are heading to the lake to go waterskiing since it's so hot outside. You're invited, you know."

"That's okay. I wouldn't be much fun today anyway."

"Suit yourself."

I heard the front door slam shut and Hunter's truck leave the driveway. So rarely was I ever left completely alone, it almost felt foreign. Usually, Matt or Jackson would be left to watch over me, but they were both busy with their families for the weekend.

Thinking about the sunshine, I decided to go outside and lie out on the grass. Maybe the heat would help to dry up my sinuses. It couldn't hurt, anyway. I grabbed a blanket off my bed and called Charlie to go out with me.

Within a few minutes, I'd created a cozy spot on the

lawn for me to lie out. Charlie had opted to rest several feet away in the shade of one of our maple trees. I listened to the chirping birds and crickets until I fell fast asleep with the warmth of the sunshine soaking into my body.

Time was not something very easy for me to gauge, but I knew something was definitely wrong. I had no idea where I was, but the feeling of something soft caressing the side of my face was definitely different. Not only that, I was freezing cold.

Moving my hand, I discovered I was completely soaked from head to toe. The feeling on my cheek was Charlie licking the water from where it dripped down my face. Just as I sat up, the sprinkler sprayed me with a fresh wash of icy water. Then it all came back into my head.

How could I have been so tired not to notice when the sprinklers came on? Groaning in dismay, I realized I'd have to get inside and dried off before my family returned. I could just imagine how they would all hover and chatter their concerns about my health if they caught me in such a state.

As soon as the hot water in the shower touched my face, I realized I wouldn't be able to hide my afternoon activity. I'm sure the sunburn was quite spectacular. I sure didn't plan this very well.

No matter how long I stayed in the shower with the scalding hot water pouring over me, I couldn't seem to get warm. When I ran out of hot water, I wrapped myself in a towel and slung my wet blanket over the shower rod so it could drip dry.

It seemed strange that such a simple activity would cause me to be so exhausted. All I could think about was putting on my pajamas and curling up in my bed. It almost seemed too much trouble just to put on clothes, but I managed.

As I lay down on my side, my peripheral vision caught sight of the pink canopy on my bed, the sunlight striking one of the sequins sewn around the edges. A smile played on my lips for the decorations my mom had given me when I was so little. I seldom thought about them since losing most of my vision, and it never occurred to me to ask to redecorate. This was my last thought as I fell asleep.

"What's wrong with her? She's burning up!" Mom said, her cool hand touching my cheek.

Lifting my hand felt like such a monstrous task, yet I managed to move enough to catch my mom's notice. I felt terrible like an elephant was sitting on my chest rather than the thin comforter. A shiver ran through me, and I wondered why I hadn't warmed up during my nap.

"I'm fine, Mom," I mumbled, straining to get the words out of my throat. "I just got a sunburn."

"No, Haley, this's more than a simple sunburn. C'mon; I'm taking you to the emergency room."

"Mom!" I moaned, dismayed with the idea of how she was overreacting to such a simple problem. "I swear I'm fine. I'm just tired."

The covers lifted from my body, allowing the cool air to wash over my body, and causing me to shiver even harder. I could feel goosebumps forming all over my skin. Mom's hands were suddenly replaced by my dad's. He lifted me from the bed as if I were still a little child and I didn't have the energy to protest.

An hour later, I was hooked up to an IV line and bundled

up on an uncomfortable hospital bed. A small win for my blindness came in the form of Charlie's warm body lying next to mine on the bed. I could hear my parents talking in the hallway with the doctor and decided to listen in because that was the only way I'd hear the unvarnished truth about my condition.

"Haley has a severe case of pneumonia. She's lucky you brought her in when you did," the doctor advised, his words carefully measured as all of them did when delivering particularly bad news.

"But how's this possible? She was fine when we left this morning," Mom argued.

"It's hard to say. She might've had symptoms which she hadn't mentioned. All I can say is her x-ray and bloodwork clearly show how hard her body is working to fight off the virus. We'll keep her overnight and reevaluate her in the morning. Try not to disturb her. The best thing for her is sleep right now."

"We're scheduled to fly to New York in six days. She'll be alright by then, right?" my dad asked.

"I wouldn't advise any trips in the near future. She's just not strong enough. Any exertions right now could set her back or cause a relapse. You'd better reschedule your plans."

"But we can't reschedule. She's been selected to participate in a research study to cure her Batten disease. She has to be there. Don't you understand?" My mom's voice rose with every sentence.

"Honey, please keep your voice down. You don't want Haley to hear, do you?"

I had to keep from scoffing at that statement. Did they

really think I wouldn't be able to hear everything they said right outside my open door? Yet, I did feel my heart breaking a little at the idea of missing out on the drug trials. I had to get better; my life depended on it.

I must have fallen asleep again, because the next time I woke up, I could feel someone holding my hand. Immediately, I noticed the familiar cologne and knew who had come to be with me. "Hey, Matt," I whispered.

"Hey! I didn't know you were awake. How're you feeling? I came as soon as I heard you were sick. What happened?"

I sighed and rolled my head on the pillow until I faced Matt's direction. "Something incredibly stupid. I fell asleep outside and got soaked by the sprinklers."

"Well, I guess that explains your spectacular sunburn. I wasn't going to say anything, but now that you've brought it up..." His hand squeezed mine playfully.

"Ha. Ha." I scoffed, starting to chuckle but ended up in a coughing fit so severe I thought I might actually pass out.

My outburst must have caught the nurse's attention because Matt was asked to leave as the hospital staff started fussing over me, propping me up, and offering ice chips. All I really wanted was to have Matt back by my side.

"I don't think you should have visitors right now, Haley," Taylor declared as she took my pulse and checked my oxygen levels.

She may have always been my favorite nurse, but right now she was getting on my nerves. "I need him, Taylor. You know how I hate being alone in the hospital. I promise I'll fall asleep if I get too tired. Please, just let him come and sit with me."

"Fine. But I'll be checking in with you regularly until my shift is over."

A smile tugged at the corners of my mouth; it was the best I could do with my limited amount of energy. Seconds later, Matt returned by my bedside, again holding my hand. "You really scared me."

"I'm sorry, Matt. This must bring back some pretty terrible memories for you. You don't have to stay, you know."

"There's nowhere I'd rather be but by your side."

"Do you think you could do me a favor?"

"Anything. Just name it. If you want a burger and fries, I'm on it."

"No, nothing like that. Could you take Charlie out to go potty?"

Matt laughed, clearly not expecting that request. He squeezed my hand playfully and answered, "I've already done that twice. He's good for now."

"Whew. I've been worried about him." I sighed, thinking about all the other problems cropping up just because my body decided to get sick right now.

"Spill it, Haley. What's wrong?"

"I'm not going to get the trial drugs."

"Don't say that, Haley."

"No, listen to me. I'm not just being dramatic. I overheard the doctor telling my parents that there's no way I can travel in six days."

"Five," Matt corrected.

Alarmed at his news, I tried to sit up and ended up in another coughing fit. This one didn't last as long, and I managed to get it under control before the nurses charged back in. "I've already lost a day?"

"Yes. But the rest did you good. You already look better, but the doctors want to keep you for another day. Once your bloodwork has a better white blood cell count, then they'll consider sending you home. They're pumping you full of antibiotics with this IV here."

"At least it's doing something good for me. I just wish they'd heat it up so it wouldn't make me cold all over." I shut my mouth. I hated sounding like a whiner and a complainer.

Matt's warm hand rubbed up and down my arm causing my flesh to ripple with chills. I could get used to this kind of attention, I much preferred it to the poking and prodding the nurses usually did whenever they touched me. "Thanks, Matt. You're the best friend ever."

"Speaking of best friends, Jackson was here earlier. He wanted to say hello, but you were still sleeping."

"I'm sorry I missed him. Where're my parents? I'm surprised they aren't hovering over me."

"Well, about that...."

"Spill it already. I promise I can handle whatever news you've got to share."

"If you're not able to travel for the trial, your parents are working on bringing the trial here."

"They'll never go for that. They've got to set up so much; it's never going to work."

"That's what your dad said. So, they're also looking to find out when the second round of trials will be held. If that doesn't work out, there's another study which is close to being released. It's possible that you'll be considered for it, based on your age. So, I don't want you to worry. There're plenty of us doing that for you. Okay?"

"No problem there. I'll just be here sleeping while the world passes by without me."

"Now you're getting the right idea."

"Tell me a story while I rest."

"Do you want to hear about Charlie when he was a puppy?"

"That'd be amazing. I bet he was the best little boy ever."

Matt chuckled, his fingers tracing patterns up across my palm. It reminded me of a game we used to play as children. "Well, Charlie used to have a thing for chewing on shoes. The first pair he ate was my mother's favorite jogging sneakers.

"You can imagine how much Mom cared for him after that. My dad teased her mercilessly until he learned how devastating it was to lose his own work shoes in the same week. Then we all learned to put them away from his ever-searching mouth."

"I'm glad he got over that habit. My family leaves their shoes everywhere." I reached over and ran my hand over Charlie's silky smooth crown then lifting one satiny ear and playing with it while he slept on. "What else?"

Matt continued to share silly little stories with me until my body decided it needed rest more than company. I never knew if he left my side or if he slept in the chair. This was the first time I didn't worry about falling asleep since I had Matt and Charlie to look after me. I could fully relax and enjoy the sweet dreams of my future.

CHAPTER THIRTEEN

It's official; I missed the drug trial because I was still battling with my bout of pneumonia. For some dumb reason, it took over two weeks for my body to fight off the virus even with all of the medical treatment I received. Now, I'm convalescing in my bedroom again, back where it all started.

I keep hearing my mom cry when she thinks I'm asleep or far enough away to not hear her. She tells me it's not my fault, but she doesn't know that it really is. I kept pushing myself all summer, enjoying my time with Matt and Jackson. We were doing everything I ever wanted to accomplish, and we documented it all. But I have to believe it wasn't all for nothing.

How can she say it wasn't my fault? Or maybe she's just trying to make me feel better. That's probably the case. If I get depressed, then it'll take me longer to get better. She needs me healthy in case another study opens up where I might be accepted.

Even Matt didn't come over as often. I don't know if my

parents made him feel guilty for his part in it, or if he just blamed himself. Either way, I missed him. Yeah, he answered my phone calls and text messages, but I missed having him by my side.

If I have to spend one more day lying in bed, I think my mind is going to crack. Already, I can feel the loose marbles rolling around in my head just waiting for the slightest opening to escape and roll right on out of me. Maybe I should let them go and then chase them down to see where they take me.

Okay, now I'm just being overly dramatic. But I am bored. There had to be some activity I could do which wouldn't overly tax me. Now that I think about it; there was the trial with the bicycle that I hadn't experimented with. For the first time in days, I was eager to do something exciting.

I grabbed up my phone and called Matt's number. He picked up on the second ring which surprised me more than I cared to admit. I had to tell him my plan before I chickened out.

"I'm going to try riding my bike today," I announced with more bravado than I actually felt.

"Really? Who's going with you? Are you sure you're strong enough?"

Hearing the same tone of concern as my parents coming out of Matt's mouth made my patience snap. "Look, I'm done with sitting around twiddling my thumbs. I'm hooking Charlie up to the bike and going for a ride. Alone if I have to!"

My finger was poised over the button to end the call. If he said one word of objection, then he was going to hear the dial tone. Okay, nobody heard dial tones anymore, but you get what I mean.

"Okay. I'll be right over. Promise me that you'll wait until I get there."

My fingers clenched around my heart-shaped pendant so tightly; I'm pretty sure the edges left permanent indents on my hand. He was going along with my plan! This was going to happen. "I promise," I managed to get out of my mouth without bursting into a shout of glee.

Matt hung up before I said another word. I flung the covers off of me, accidentally covering Charlie with the bulk of it. As soon as I felt him struggling to free himself, I pulled them off of him. He jumped off the bed, eager to go wherever I wanted to go.

"We're heading outside, Charlie!" I announced proudly.

"Oh, yeah? Where're you off to in such a hurry," Hunter asked from my doorway.

I jumped about two feet into the air. Somehow, he had managed to sneak up on me. It was easier these days since he'd stopped wearing his horrid cologne after breaking up with his girlfriend. Now I couldn't smell him a mile away, so he became stealthier. I'd have to pay more attention now that I was onto his new tactic for surveilling me.

"I'm going to learn how to ride my bike again. Get out your camera, Hunter; this's going to be quite the adventure." I snapped Charlie's lead into place and boldly walked out of my room.

"Do you even know where the apparatus is?" Hunter asked.

"Nope, but I'm betting that you do. I'll be waiting out by the garage. Matt's coming over to assist." I'm pretty sure my excitement was fueling my energy right now because I wasn't feeling the least bit fatigued. I walked through the living room and heard my mom talking on the phone. Just as I suspected, she paused in her conversation to talk to me.

"Haley, honey. What're you doing out of bed?" she asked, her voice tinged with worry.

"I'm going outside to ride my bike."

"I have to go," Mom said to whoever was on the other end of the line. I heard the phone drop onto the table, and her chair legs squeal in protest as she stood up too fast. "Haley, you don't want to overdo it. Maybe, you should just go sit on the lawn. You like to do that, right?"

By now, she had reached me at the front door. I wasn't about to be dissuaded from my present course of action. Instead of docilely agreeing with her, my temper overflowed. "No, Mom. If I have to spend another second in my room, I'll go crazy. I need some fresh air and some time with my friends. If you want to watch, that's fine, but I'm going to give this a try. After all, it was your suggestion to begin with, right?"

"Yes, but that was before…"

"Before what, Mom? When you thought I was going to get the drug trial and live? I want to live right now. Right this moment. Matt and Hunter are both meeting me outside. I've got to go."

"But…" Mom weakly protested.

I walked out the door with Charlie. Behind me, I heard Hunter saying, "I'll watch out for her." I grinned, thinking this had actually happened better than I thought it would. Either Mom was really worried about me, or she thought this might help me because she was keeping her objections to herself for the time being.

I just hoped I didn't fail so epically bad that she would rub it in with me later. People always said learning to ride a bike was so easy to pick back up again. Hopefully, this would be true for me as well.

A vehicle was coming up our driveway, so I kept myself to the edge of the lawn. As soon as I heard the music playing from inside, I knew it was Matt. For some reason, I'd thought he would ride his bike over, but I was just thankful he was here at all. Who knew all I had to do was threaten to do something drastic to get people moving into action. I should have done this sooner. Well, except I really didn't have the energy any earlier than right now.

I heard Hunter talking with Matt over by the garage. Somehow, he'd managed to sneak by me again. I was losing my touch. Charlie unerringly led me over to be with the boys. "Well; what's the plan?"

"We've almost got your bike rigged up. I think Matt's right that we should head over to the park where there're some wide bike paths for you to practice on. Our driveway isn't very bike-friendly, you know."

"True. But this better not be some scheme you two have cooked up to keep me from trying!"

"We wouldn't dare!" Matt teased, leaning over and kissing my cheek.

"Don't try to butter me up, mister. I'm onto you."

"I'm not up to anything except getting you ready to go. I brought over a couple of other things for you, just in case."

"Like what?"

"Nope. I'm not sharing until we get to the park. You can ride with me while Hunter takes your bike over in the back of his truck."

"Hmm. Okay. But you both sound suspicious to me." I turned and had Charlie lead me to Matt's car. I let myself into the passenger seat with Charlie on the floorboard between my feet. There wasn't much room with him, but I preferred having him close at hand.

A few minutes later, Matt jumped into the driver's seat and turned on the car. Immediately, the radio blasted out its tunes, practically deafening me on the spot. Almost as fast as it started, Matt flipped the radio off. "Sorry about that."

"I still don't know how you aren't deaf," I teased.

"Lots of practice, I guess. Are you sure you're up for this? I mean, you don't have anything to prove, you know."

I folded my arms and refused to give him the satisfaction of an answer. He knew not to push me past this point, proving it by remaining silent and starting the car. Instantly, my mood shifted into exuberance as a huge grin spread across my face. I'm sure I seemed bi-polar, but I was tired of everyone expecting so little of me. I needed them to trust in my own judgment for once.

By the time we reached the park a few minutes later, the adrenaline was coursing through my veins. I'm pretty sure if I'd held my hands out that my fingers would be shaking like a leaf. But nothing was going to stop me from attempting to ride my bike. Even Charlie seemed more animated than usual, although he was probably just picking up on my excitement.

As it turned out, Matt's additions to this adventure included a helmet as well as knee and elbow pads. "I'm surprised you didn't find me a sumo wrestling outfit to cushion my entire body," I commented as I buckled the helmet under my chin.

"Trust me; if I would've had more time, I would've gotten one," Matt answered, chuckling at my expense.

"Ha. Ha. I'm sure I look fairly ridiculous already. Are you getting all this on film, Hunter?"

"You bet. You're going to do great. Break a leg, kid," he cheerfully replied.

"Dude, did you have to say that? You know what could happen to her, right?"

"Um, I'm right here boys. I may be blind, but there's nothing wrong with my hearing. Besides, with all this protective gear, I doubt I'll manage to even get a scrape let alone fall hard enough to break something."

"Oh, no! Now you've gone and jinxed yourself!" Matt groaned theatrically.

"Enough fooling around. When're we going to get rolling already?"

"Right now. But Haley, please don't fight me on this. For Charlie's sake, okay?" Matt asked, standing right beside me with his hand on my arm.

I didn't like how this was sounding, but I also didn't want them to pull the plug on my adventure. I nodded and said, "Sure. What do you have in mind?"

"I'm going to hold onto your bike while you go slowly. That way Charlie will get the feel of it, and you'll begin to remember how to balance on your own."

"Sounds great!"

"It does?" Matt asked, his tone clearly surprised by my easy acceptance.

"Look, Matt. I wanted to ride a bike today. I don't have any desire to end up back in the hospital. I'm glad you want to help me; and to be honest, I was slightly concerned about how I'd manage without your assistance."

"Oh, thank goodness, Haley." Matt pulled me into a hug, his relief evident in the rush of air he let out of his lungs right next to my ear.

I patted his back in appreciation, but also because I enjoyed the return of our physical contact. This was something I missed more than I believed possible. My nervousness returned in full-force as soon as he pulled away. I knew my time was now. I'd either learn to ride or fail miserably while trying. You may have learned by now: I'm not a quitter.

We took things slowly with Matt steadying my bike like a father would hold their toddler's bike. I didn't care. I was outside, trying something new, and spending time with the people I loved. With each new pass, I gained confidence in my ability to balance and with Charlie's ability to guide me away from obstacles.

And my faithful brother caught it all on film. I hoped this video would encourage disabled people all over the world to face their fears head-on and try new things. If nothing else, I wanted my life to inspire people and to make a difference in their lives. That's what everyone wants, right?

I had no idea how our activity had drawn the attention of the people at the park. By the time I managed to do my one and only solo trek on the trail, the crowd had cheered me on. At first, the sound caught me off guard and made me wobble dangerously, but I regained my focus and kept going. I was doing it. I was riding my bike alone, and it felt amazing.

When I came to a stop at Charlie's insistence, I felt familiar arms wrap around me. "You were amazing, Haley!" my mom praised. "I knew you could do it."

Now she'd gone and done it; she made me start to cry. Although, these were tears of happiness because she had come to watch me. She allowed me to struggle and almost get hurt, all without uttering a sound. I'm sure it'd been hard on her, but she always had faith in my ability to do whatever I set my mind to. She just kept proving it to me all the time, and I loved her so much for it.

In order to lighten the mood I said, "Well, it was more successful than taking the goats for a walk in the park, at least."

A second later, Mom burst out laughing. "I'd forgotten all about that. Yes, it's true. It looks like you get to come home without a scratch. To celebrate, I think we should order Chinese takeout for dinner tonight. What do you say, Haley?"

"You took the idea straight out of my head. I've worked up quite the appetite tonight. How soon do you think we can get it? After all, I don't want to fall asleep before it arrives." I laughed like I was joking, but it crossed my mind that it was a definite possibility now that my adrenaline had given up.

"It should be arriving at the same time as we do, if we leave right now," Mom answered.

In record time, we packed everything up and headed back home. Matt came inside with us, sitting down beside me at the table and holding my hand just the way I liked. Following our tradition, Mom passed out the fortune cookies, and I cracked mine open. I held it out to her and asked, "What does mine say?"

She took it from me and read, "Great things come in invisible packages. You will be delighted."

Instantly I grinned and replied, "Awesome! That means they'll cure Batten."

"Yes, my love! Let's pray they do," Mom answered, her voice full of hope for my prediction.

CHAPTER FOURTEEN

I don't know how he did it, but I shouldn't be surprised; Grandpa managed to get me into another drug trial. He must have called in several favors in order to make this happen so swiftly. This one was scheduled five days from now, and it's in California. At least I wouldn't have to expend all my energy traveling across the country.

"Isn't this the best news ever, Haley?" my mom asked as she hugged me tightly to her. She barely withheld her tears, fighting valiantly to keep herself together for my sake.

I could hear it in her voice and feeling through her hands where she clutched my arms. Before I could respond, my mom let go, and my grandfather took her place. He pulled me into his embrace and whispered into my ear, "I'm not going to lose another grandchild. I'd do anything for you, Haley."

"I know, Grandpa." I patted his back, letting him know I appreciated his efforts. My longevity was a testament to his efforts since he'd been the one to start the fundraising foundation for the research. So much good had come from it so far, and I knew my family was making a difference in the study of Batten disease.

"How are we going to have enough time to get all the testing done that I'm sure they're going to need?" I asked as soon as Grandpa let me go.

"That's the best part, Haley," Mom answered. "They're able to use the test results from your latest round. The only thing they need from you is current bloodwork once we get there. Isn't that great!"

Wow, it almost seemed too good to be true. Already my wheels were turning, planning what I needed to pack. I must have spaced out a bit, because my mom grabbed my arm, catching my attention. "Yeah, Mom. That's great. I'm going to go call Matt."

Instead of waiting for her response, I turned around and rushed back to my room where I'd left my phone on my nightstand. As soon as he picked up the line, I announced, "I got into another trial. Please tell me you'll be able to come with me on short notice."

"How short are we talking? You know school starts soon."

"That's the best part, not only is it in California, it's in five days."

"But that's your birthday, Haley. Hold that thought; I'm coming over."

I held the phone in my hand, excited to have Matt so close by that he could be here in minutes. It was hard to believe I had forgotten my birthday was right around the corner and even harder to believe that Matt would remember it so readily. I wondered if he had planned some surprise for me and now I'd messed it up with my grandpa's news. That was probably it.

Before I imagined it could be possible, I heard Matt's car pull into our driveway. Usually, he would just jog over, but he must've wanted to get here even faster.

He usually came into my room first thing, so I found it odd that he stopped in the kitchen to talk with my mom and Grandpa instead. I could hear him animatedly talking until they noticed me coming. Something didn't seem quite right, but I didn't want any discord right now, so I opted to let it go.

Matt came over and kissed me a on the cheek in greeting. He seemed more distant than usual, something I didn't like much. "I can't stay, Haley. I'll call you later, okay?"

He led me outside before I even had a chance to object. "What? I don't understand. What happened with my mom and Grandpa?"

"Nothing, Haley. I've got an idea, but I don't want to say anything in case I can't get it to work out. Since your trial is in five days, we don't have a minute to spare in getting everything in order. I gotta go." He hugged me faster than he normally would before he left me standing alone and terribly confused.

I turned around and marched back into the house, my scowl a clear indication I wasn't happy. Based on the sound of their voices, my family hadn't moved from the kitchen, so I marched back in there. "What did you say to him?"

"Look, Haley, we can't wait around for Matt to clear his schedule. If he can't come with us, then we'll just have to make arrangements for you to call him once we're there. It's pretty simple, really."

"Easy for you to say. I need him there, Mom. That's a non-negotiable." I stomped back to my room, slamming the door behind me. I hated it when people were making decisions for me behind my back, then having the audacity to tell me it was for my own good. I'm pretty sure I know what's good for me.

Not wanting to hear anything more anyone might have to say to me, I grabbed up my earbuds and shoved them into my ears. I turned up my music louder than normal and sat down on the floor next to my bed where Charlie had taken up residence. He snuck his muzzle onto my lap, and I absently began stroking his back. Charlie always knew exactly what I needed, and I loved him more for it.

ಸಾ ೧೩೮೦ ೦೩

"Happy birthday, Haley," Matt said as he entered my room. He seemed pretty cheerful for someone who had a whole day of traveling ahead of him. But that was just how he was all the time.

After planting a smoking hot kiss on my lips which left me nearly speechless, Matt refused to give me any details of our day, but he did assure me that he was coming with me on this trip. He probably noticed my stubborn streak setting in and decided he better share that point or else I'd refuse to go at all.

My packed bag stood next to my bedroom door, and a bout of nerves struck me out of the blue. Charlie pressed up against my side as if he knew I was starting to panic. Automatically, my fingers pressed into his thick hair until I could feel his flesh beneath. I massaged him and relaxed myself at the same time.

"Okay, we're ready to go, Haley," Matt announced as he came back to my room. I heard the snapping of the handle being extended on my bag and knew that Matt had decided to take it for me. "All we're missing is you. Are you okay?"

"Sure; I guess. This's going to be a huge change in my life, and I'm just a little nervous."

Matt's hand found mine, his fingers twining with mine and giving me a little squeeze. "You'll do great. Besides, I've got something really special planned, so think about that instead. Okay?"

"What is it?" I pressed, hoping he'd accidentally tell me something.

"Nice try. Now, quit stalling. We've got a plane to catch."

"I hate the long drive to the airport. I think that's possibly worse than the flight itself." I knew I was complaining, but it was just how I deflected from feeling nervous.

About ten minutes later, the car came to a stop, and the engine turned off. "What's going on? Why did we stop?" I asked. I turned my head to try to identify our location. None of the blurry shapes around me looked familiar.

"You ask too many questions, Haley. Just trust me on this, okay? In a few minutes, you'll have your first surprise," Matt said as he opened my door and helped me out.

He was talking away from me, and it made me suspicious. "Are you filming this?"

"Of course. We want everyone to enjoy this journey with you. I thought you wanted that, too."

"Well, yes. But please tell me you're not using a selfie-stick."

Matt chuckled, purposely not answering me.

"You are using one. Oh, Matt, we're going to make such a spectacle of ourselves."

"Since when have you ever cared about that? What we're doing is more important than anything these onlookers are doing. Besides, I got a special selfie-stick. This one doesn't show up in the video footage."

"Ah, I guess that should make all the difference. Okay, fine. Take me to my first surprise. Like you kept telling me all morning; we don't have time to mess around."

"Now you're talking. Your chariot awaits."

He led me across a hard, flat surface. The scents around me were unlike anything I'd smelled before. Maybe we were in a parking garage? Although, I didn't know of one this close to our house. A parking lot, maybe?

"Did you plan a different car for us to drive in?"

"Nope. Even better."

"Hmm." Matt knew I liked playing guessing games, but this one was really stumping me.

"Okay, step up now," Matt advised. "There're three steps slightly taller than normal and then a platform at the top."

As soon as I reached the platform, I still had no idea where I was. Then my mother's voice came from my right-hand side. "Isn't this amazing, Haley? Matt arranged for us to fly to San Francisco in a private jet. Now we won't have to worry about airport security or any issues with getting Charlie onto the flight."

My eyebrows must have risen to my hairline. I did not

expect anything this cool. I turned around just in time to bump into Matt as Charlie pushed past me to lead me into the airplane cabin. "How did you do this, Matt?"

"It's my aunt's airplane. She was thrilled to offer it to us."

"That's pretty epic. Where do I sit?" This was turning into quite the adventure, much better than anything I could have imagined.

"Just over here," he answered, taking my hand and pulling me forward.

He settled me in an oversized, leather chair, unlike any airline seat I'd ever experienced. Charlie took up his spot at my feet, his stomach resting over the tips of my toes. Matt reached over and helped to get me buckled up before he sat down in the seat next to me.

I still couldn't believe we were actually taking a trip together. This was one of my secret desires, but now it was becoming a reality. Of course, I couldn't say anything to Matt about what this meant to me without sounding completely stupid, so I kept my mouth shut.

"When do we leave?" I asked instead.

"Just as soon as the crew gets our bags into the luggage compartment."

"It sounds like you know all about how this goes. This isn't your first time; is it?"

"No, but this will definitely be my favorite time."

"Why's that?"

"Because I've never traveled with a girlfriend before. You're what makes this trip special."

"Is that how you think of me? As your girlfriend?"

"Uh, duh. I thought we'd already established that before.

I don't go around kissing random girls, you know."

I bit my bottom lip as my cheeks heated up. Turning my head, I grinned at his admission. Since we were being so honest right now, I thought I'd ask the question which had been bothering me for so long. "If that's how you feel about me, then why did you spend so much time away from me while I had pneumonia?"

"Maybe because you wouldn't have been sick in the first place if it hadn't been for me. I pushed you too hard and tired you out. I should've been taking better care of you, and I almost lost you like I lost my brother. I stayed away because I thought it would help."

"I swear, boys can be so stupid sometimes. My getting sick didn't have anything to do with you, well not directly anyway. I chose to go out; I knew I was pushing myself. But I was doing it for me, not for you. Promise me that you won't leave me like that again. It was the worst time of my life."

Matt reached over and held my face between his hands. In the most sincere voice I'd ever heard him use, he said, "Haley, I promise to be everything you need from now on. I'll be by your side whenever you want me there because I love you."

"You love me?"

"Couldn't you tell?"

Rather than make more of a fool of myself than I already had, I pressed forward until my lips met his. I'm pretty sure my reaction startled him, but he kissed me back for a split second before pulling away. I was about to protest when someone spoke from the front of the plane.

"Everyone, please make sure your seatbelts are fastened.

We've closed the cabin door and are prepared for takeoff."

"This is it!" I announced into the silence. My family laughed at my enthusiasm as the engines fired up and the airplane began moving. We were really on our way.

So much had changed in such a short amount of time. My predictions for the perfect summer were coming true. Matt squeezed my hand as we started rolling faster up the runway.

Here I was, traveling with my boyfriend who had just declared his love for me. I'd found romance, and he had created the most special memories for me, even better than I could have imagined on my own. My life couldn't get any better than this moment right now.

Chapter Fifteen

"This must be your Haley," a woman said as soon as Matt, and I stepped off the airplane. I felt Matt leave my side and wondered who this woman could be. Matt's next words clued me in.

"Yes, Aunt Chrissy. Let me introduce you," he answered.

Matt returned to my side and pulled me forward. He took my hand and offered it to his aunt. "Haley, this's my Aunt Chrissy who arranged the airplane and a place for all of us to stay."

I firmly grasped her hand, simply because I detested a wimpy handshake, and smiled in her direction. "It was an amazing surprise. I can't thank you enough for your thoughtfulness."

"Oh, that's okay, honey. Don't think anything of it. We also donate our flight time with Angel Flights West, so this was actually just a routine flight for us. But I am glad you enjoyed the flight.

"You're going to love my condominium in Mission Bay.

It's right on the waterfront, and it's so close to where your research study is being held; I couldn't have planned it any better if I'd tried!"

"Wow, I had no idea." I turned and scowled in Matt's direction. "Someone hasn't shared any details with me, so I find I'm at quite the disadvantage!"

"Oops," Chrissy said, her tone playful. "I guess I won't say anything about tonight's plans then."

"No, we won't be discussing that right now," Matt interjected quickly. "Let's get Haley and Charlie settled in the car and then we can be on our way."

I got the distinct impression Matt was trying to keep something from me, but if he wanted to surprise me, then I decided not to put up too much of a fuss. As soon as I sat down in the car with Charlie sitting up on the seat beside me, his panting in my ear made it more difficult for me to hear Matt speaking with his aunt.

"Were you able to arrange the special event tonight?"

"Yes, dear. Oh, good. I see you brought…"

"Shh. Don't say anything. She may not admit it, but I'm convinced Haley's hearing is amazing, and I don't want to give anything away."

"My lips are sealed then. It's going to be so much fun, though!"

Chrissy's gentle laughter made a smile come to my own lips. Whatever Matt had planned for me tonight also included something else from my house. What that could be, I had no clue. At least I wouldn't have to wait too long to find out.

A few minutes later, everyone was in the vehicle, and we were on our way. According to Matt, his Aunt Chrissy had many houses in the area which she used depending on what was happening in her various businesses. One thing kept coming back to my mind, so I decided to ask about it.

"What was she saying about Angel Flight West? What's that all about?"

"Oh, it's a dream of mine to work with them one day when I'm old enough and have my pilot's license. It's an organization which arranges flights for medical patients who might not have the means to get the proper treatment without free transportation."

"But I'm sure my parents could've afforded our flights, though," I insisted, although I imagined this might have actually been a blessing considering the fights I'd recently heard about paying for the medical bills.

"Oh, no. She did this just because I asked for a favor. She knows how much I love flying and she was more than happy to help. Besides, I think she really wanted to meet you."

"Why? Do you talk about me all the time or something?"

"Of course."

That response gave me a reason to pause. It never occurred to me that people would be talking about me. I mean, I was just an ordinary girl. Blind, but still ordinary. What could he have possibly talked about which would cause his aunt to want to meet me?

"You should see the look on your face, Haley. Why is it so hard to believe I'd talk about you with my family? After all, we did spend an amazing summer together. Also, Aunt Chrissy has watched all of our adventures on the YouTube channel. She's quite impressed with how brave you are."

"What am I supposed to say to that?"

"Nothing."

"Okay," I whispered to myself. "So, what's the plan for today?"

Mom turned around from the front seat and said, "You've got your initial appointment with the doctor at one. After that, you've got the rest of the night free. If everything goes as planned, then your first dose will be administered tomorrow."

"Ah," I answered. I wondered how much research my mom had done on all of this. Probably more than I cared to know. I turned to face Matt and said, "So, you've got something planned for me this evening, right?"

"I knew you'd hear us. Yes. And I'm going to need you to wear something nice."

"What if I didn't pack anything appropriate? After all, I was only expecting to be visiting the doctor."

"Oh, I made sure your mom had something appropriate for you."

"So Mom's in on this, too, huh?"

"Don't try it, Haley. You're not wheedling any information out of us, so you might as well give up now. Just enjoy the journey."

Matt slung his arm across my shoulders and pulled me into his side. Charlie's head popped up from where he'd been resting on the seat between us. I gave him several pats on the head before he settled back down for the rest of the ride.

※ ✿ ❀ ✿

After a quick tour of our accommodations, Matt took me to check out the greenspace area as well as the waterfront. As soon as we stepped outside, I could smell the water nearby. It definitely smelled different than when we were on the Oregon coast, but I still enjoyed the variance.

We sat down on one of the benches near the water and listened to the birds. For such a busy city, this seemed like a small piece of paradise. "I didn't know you wanted to learn how to fly."

"Yeah, ever since I was little. One of my aunt's businesses involves rescue flights with both airplanes and helicopters. I've been out with them on lots of flights. It was easier when we lived closer, though."

"Do you think your family will move back here, then?" Just saying it out loud made my heart thud darkly in my chest. I hated the idea of him leaving, but I also didn't want to be the cause of him losing his dream. I'd just have to be fine with whatever he decided.

"We talked about it, but we decided I'd finish out my senior year before we made any decisions. After all, my dad just got transferred to his job, so they wanted to give it a chance."

"Oh, well, that's good. I'm glad you'll be hanging around for a while."

"Hanging around? Haley, don't you get it by now? I told you I loved you on the airplane and you think I'm just hanging around? Even if my parents moved back to California today, I'd figure out a way to stay in Oregon to be near you."

"Oh." What could I say to that? I really needed help with this whole romance thing. The books I listened to made it sound so easy to fall in love where everything became sunshine and roses. Nobody ever talked about the awkward conversations and the confusion over how to react during times like this. Maybe I should find the Romance for Dummies book and listen to that!

"We should head back so you can get ready for your appointment," Matt suggested as he stood up and pulled Charlie and me along with him.

ဢ ⌘ ଔ

The waiting room had the same antiseptic smell as any hospital I'd ever visited. It didn't do anything for my nerves, but at least I had Matt and Charlie sitting beside me this time. My mom had left us to go fill out the paperwork at the receptionist's desk.

I could feel the time drawing closer as I heard snippets of conversation from the receptionist. My hand automatically rose for my fingers to play with my pendant. It had been with me at every doctor's appointment, and I just knew it brought me luck so far.

Something was wrong, though. My fingers searched in vain before the truth became abundantly clear: my necklace was gone. "Oh, no!" I cried out into the nearly silent waiting room.

"What is it?" Matt asked just as urgently.

I'm sure there was something terrible going on with me physically, but how could I say my necklace was part of my mental health? "My necklace! It's gone, Matt! We've got to find it right now. Do you see it anywhere?"

"It's okay, Haley. Calm down. I'm looking as we

speak."

My breathing came faster as I began to panic in earnest. This could not be happening right now. Surely, Matt would find it on the floor in front of me, and all would be well.

"Haley Vallem," a nurse called from the far side of the room.

"That's us, Haley," my mom said from right in front of me.

"I can't, Mom. I lost my necklace. I can't go in there without it."

"Nonsense, Haley. We can't keep the doctors waiting just because you lost your silly pendant. I'm sure it'll turn up."

Tears began forming in my eyes. This was my worst nightmare. I'd never been to a doctor's appointment without my pendant and now was not the time to find out if it made all the difference. I needed all the luck I could get, especially now.

"Haley, listen to me," Matt's calm voice began, "I promise we'll find your necklace. It's got to be here in the office, the car, or the condo. We'll check everywhere and make sure you have it for your appointment tomorrow."

"That's right, honey. The doctor only needs to interview you today. You're not starting your treatment until tomorrow. That's when you'll need your necklace. C'mon, Haley."

I knew I was acting foolishly, but it hurt too much to think the necklace might be well and truly lost. I wiped the tears from my cheeks and stood up. With a deep breath to clear my head, I nodded. I knew they'd follow up on their promises. I didn't really need the luck until the next day anyway. We'd find my necklace and all would be well. This desperate mantra kept playing through my head as I followed my mom and the nurse into the doctor's office.

~ ~~~ ~

My distraction should have been quite obvious, but the doctor kept talking as if this were normal for his test subjects. Luckily, my mom answered all the questions for me once she realized I was too preoccupied to do so myself. Matt had stayed out in the lobby to keep searching, but I had the worst feeling inside my soul that something had gone wrong, or was about to.

"Okay, so I guess we'll be seeing you tomorrow morning at ten. It was nice meeting you both."

"Thank you," I managed to mumble as my mom took my elbow and led me out of the room.

"Get it together, Haley," she whispered to me. "It's just a necklace; it's not the end of the world. Besides, Matt probably has it for you in the waiting room."

That must not have been true since Matt came up to me and handed Charlie's harness to me. I couldn't wait for him to try to come up with some excuse. "Well? Did you find it?"

"No, Haley. The staff even helped me search the entire lobby. It's not here, but I called your dad, and he's looking around the condo. Hopefully, he'll have good news for us when we get home. I'll also be looking in the car on the drive back. We'll find it, Haley. I know it's important for you to have it for your appointment tomorrow."

I stepped outside into the sunshine, but the warmth did

little to heal the pain I felt growing inside me. That was the first gift Jackson had ever given me. I'd treasured it for the past eleven years, and yet I might have carelessly lost it on the most important day of my life.

So dark were my thoughts that the drive back to the condo was just a blur. The driver pulled up to the front of the condo and waited patiently while Matt diligently searched every crack and crevice of the back where we'd been sitting. Coming up empty-handed, our last hope rested completely on my dad's search.

"Honestly, Haley. You'd think you were ten years old with how you're acting right now," Mom criticized as we rode the elevator up to the penthouse. As soon as the doors opened, Mom called out, "Oh, thank heavens!"

"What is it, Matt? Please tell me Dad found my necklace!" I grabbed Matt's arm in desperation of getting the right answer. I felt him lift his arm.

"Turn around, Haley," he directed.

In the next instant, I felt the cold metal of the pendant backing begin to warm up against my flesh. "Oh!" I cried out, my fingers confirming this was indeed my lost heart as I identified the small nick in the side.

"Where was it?" Matt asked my dad.

"I found it under the bench out by the water. I was getting pretty desperate, but then a flash of sun caught it just right and there it was. Just like magic. How lucky was that?"

"It's the luckiest ever, Dad. Thank you for finding it." I stepped forward and hugged him tightly. I didn't bother trying to stop my tears of joy from falling onto his shoulder. He had no idea how much this simple piece of jewelry meant to me, but he knew it was important.

Matt patted me on the back and said, "Now that you have that back, maybe we can work on getting you ready for our outing this afternoon."

With a considerably lightened heart, I happily nodded. Everything would be perfect from now on. I was ready for whatever Matt had in mind for my surprise tonight.

Chapter Sixteen

"You look amazing, Haley," Matt told me as I stepped out of the bedroom where my mom played dress-up on me with my clothes and hair. I had no idea what I was wearing as nobody allowed me the opportunity to look, but I suspected it was something my mom had purchased in the last couple of days on one of her mystery outings.

"Thanks," I replied, not really knowing what to do or say next. Charlie saved me from myself as he came and sat down at my feet and leaned against my leg. "I'm ready to go whenever you are."

Matt came forward and took my hand so it rested on the crook of his arm. The three of us left the condo and walked outside in the sunshine. Initially, I'd thought we'd go somewhere in the car, but Matt steered us in the opposite direction once we got to the lobby. I had no idea where we were going.

Soon enough, I recognized the scent of the waterfront and relaxed. He must've wanted to go for a walk. As tired as I'd been lately, I hoped it would be a short one. Matt seemed more in tune with me than I realized because he stopped shortly after my thought.

"Sit down on the ground right here," he directed.

I frowned at his strange request. We'd just got dressed up, and now he wanted to sit on the grass? As soon as my hand touched down, I realized someone had put down a blanket, and I began to guess as to our next activity. "Are we having a picnic?"

"Good guess. I noticed you didn't eat much earlier and thought you'd probably appreciate something."

"Yeah, I never can eat before a doctor's appointment. I just dread them. And about today..." my fingers fiddled with the wrinkles in the cloth beneath me as I organized my thoughts, "I'm sorry for getting so crazy when I thought I lost my necklace. I know it's silly, but I've always worn it to every doctor's appointment. It makes me think it gives me good luck."

"Hey, don't worry about it, Haley. I understand. Trust me; I totally get it. Although, your mom seemed pretty peeved with you."

"Nah, it didn't really have anything to do with me; she's just afraid. She tries to hide it, but these appointments scare her to death. It's part of the reason she does so much research; she hopes it'll ease some of her anxiety about the unknown."

We finished eating our lunch and ended up lying out on the blanket, soaking up the warmth of the sun while holding hands. Suddenly, I heard a familiar sound and lifted my head to listen better. "Do I hear a goat?" I asked, really thinking I must be wrong.

"What?" Matt asked. I heard him shift his body until he sat up. "Yep. I guess there're all kinds of people out here. There's a lady coming our way, and she has a pygmy goat on a leash. Craziest thing!"

"It's not that crazy. We used to have goats, and they're really smart."

"You know, I remembered you made some comment about taking the goats to the park. With the way your mom laughed about it, makes me think there's quite a story behind it."

"Definitely. When I was about nine, we took the goats and our dogs to the park, and there was a dog park right next to it. All of the dogs swarmed the goats to the point we had to get out of there. So we thought it'd be better to walk along the walking trails instead.

"Everything was going great until some lady didn't have her pit bull on a leash and the dog's hunting drive kicked in and attacked the goats. Mom and Dad were frantically trying to get the dog's jaws unlatched from Fred's face.

"Dad finally got the goat free, and the dog's owner finally showed up, with no leash in sight, mind you. She didn't even apologize as she grabbed her dog. We began herding up the goats when the dog broke loose from her and began charging toward us.

"Mom slipped and fell, causing one of our dogs to think she was injured so she tried to defend her. Somehow our dog's collar got hooked with the pit bull's collar which didn't slow him down much. The lady's dog managed to grab our other goat's back leg and began shaking her. It managed to get the collars unhooked, which was good.

"Dad ran over and leaped onto the pit bull like he was

falling on an IED in a war zone and he screamed 'Go! Go! Run to the truck!' So some strangers picked up the goats and started running while Mom still had our dogs' leashes in her hand and we all made it back to the truck before another attack could happen.

"Both Hunter and I were crying because we felt like it was our fault because we wanted to bring the goats. Mom and Dad took us home, and we cleaned up the goats. They only had little puncture wounds, but it was so scary.

"I joked with Mom at the park that I fared better than the goats. I came away from my bike riding without any injuries."

"Wow, your poor goats. Were they afraid of dogs after that?"

"No, it didn't even seem to phase them."

"What happened with the lady?"

"Nothing, she just walked away like nothing happened. Some people just shouldn't have dogs they can't control. Don't get me wrong; I don't think there's anything wrong with pit bulls, they just need to have responsible owners who understand their nature and are willing and able to correct them before it gets out of hand. That lady had no idea what to do."

"We should probably get going. We've got lots to do yet," Matt announced cryptically. "Let me help you up."

I held out my hand, and Matt pulled me to my feet beside him. Charlie stayed right next to me as we began walking. I tried to slow him down and asked, "What about our stuff? Shouldn't we…"

"It's taken care of. Don't worry about it, Haley. This afternoon is all about you."

※ ⌘ ☙

Boy, he wasn't kidding! Matt had planned so many activities for us; it almost made my head spin. It started out at the nearby aquarium where we were able to touch all of the creatures. I was in sensory heaven!

Next was a narrated bus tour of the city. I got to hear all about the history of the city while the people around us snapped picture after picture, exclaiming about different things which caught their attention.

The bus let us off near our next stop. We only had to walk about a block before Matt said, "We're going here to this museum."

I'm sure my look was comical. In my experience, museums were dedicated to displays to look at which would not be of interest to me at all. But I should've had more faith in him. This was a musical museum where we got to interact with different devices to make so many sounds I'd never seen or felt before.

Once we finished there, we grabbed a trolley car to take us a couple of blocks to a little restaurant. I could smell the fresh-baked bread even before the trolley stopped and it made my mouth water. Matt took my hand, and we walked into the building.

Something seemed different about this place. There didn't seem to be any tables for customers which caused me to wonder if I'd gotten my ideas crossed because I was hungry again.

"Ah, so are we ready for our cooking lesson?" A woman asked as we stopped at a counter.

I laughed at this idea. Matt must not have heard about my disastrous adventures in the culinary arts. "I think I'll just listen in while you guys handle it."

"Nope, not a chance, Haley. This isn't like anything you've experienced before. Everything here is designed for visually impaired clients. Come on; give it a try."

This had me intrigued. I'd never heard of anything like it. "Sure!" I agreed, already wondering what we'd be making and hoping it would be quick and easy. "I'm starved; let's get going!"

Charlie curled up in a ball on the floor and promptly fell asleep. Matt and I spent the next thirty minutes trying out everything in the kitchen. With a lot of laughter and a little bit of messiness, we managed to put together a pretty fancy dinner. There were even some leftovers for Charlie who perked up as soon as the food was served.

"Well, the evening's not over yet. We still have one more stop to make before we call it a night. Are you up for it?" Matt announced suddenly.

I grinned at his eagerness. "This has been the best afternoon ever, Matt." I stood up from my chair and held out my hand to him. He came to stand in front of me, and I put my hands behind his neck and pulled him toward me. "Thank you for everything." The next few minutes were lost to both of us as our lips touched and time ceased to exist.

ಸಾ ಲ್ಯಾ ಇಂ

Did I forget to mention that the selfie-stick was a constant companion during all of our adventures? Oh, yes, it was like having another person tagging along, but I didn't mind in the least. After all, I'd been the one to suggest documenting my life so many years ago. Why stop now just because I'm having a romantic encounter?

Matt's final surprise ended up leading us into a dark warehouse. Only the sound of our footsteps echoing off the walls could be heard as Matt walked confidently along. At least both he and Charlie could see fine; I was the only one to wonder if this was a good idea.

He led me to a seat in the middle of the floor and said, "Take a seat."

"What's going on?" This certainly wasn't what I'd been expecting for the final event of the evening. Maybe a moonlight walk by the waterfront, but not an abandoned warehouse.

Matt came to kneel in front of me, causing my heart to beat wildly in my chest. There was no way he was going to ask me to marry him. We were only seventeen, after all. So what was this all about?

"Remember that new song you wrote?"

"Yes. That one is for my mom. What about it?"

"I wanted you to play it in a place where the acoustics are really good, so that I can record it for you. Will you do that for me?"

"Okay," I slowly answered, thinking this seemed strange, even for Matt. I heard a little commotion and then felt a cello being put in front of me. Then it dawned on me; this was my cello. This was the item Matt had brought from my house. Then he handed me my bow, and I chuckled at his deviousness in pulling this off. My whole family must have been behind it all along.

"Haley?"

"Yeah?"

"Promise me that you'll keep playing and singing all the way to the end without stopping. I'm almost out of room on my camera so we only have time for one take."

"Sure. No problem. Just tell me when to start." I shifted the cello until it was exactly right in front of me and lifted my arms into the ready position.

"Now."

My fingers knew exactly what to do; the music flowed through me just like it had at the museum. Now I realized what Matt had been doing all day. He wanted me to have a day full of sensory experiences all leading up to this one. When the moment came, I opened my mouth and began singing the words which honored my mother's love and her beautiful spirit.

So into my own music had I become, I failed to realize more music had started all around me. It felt like I was playing in a symphony. Then a spotlight turned on, and my peripheral vision caught sight of dozens of people all playing their own instruments.

They were all playing *my* music. Tears came to my eyes as I realized Matt had given me my biggest and most hidden dream. I was playing on stage with a professional orchestra. Even as I began to get nervous, I tamped down my fear and let the rush of adrenaline feed into my flow of music instead. This was my moment to own.

When the last notes faded away, the thunderous sound of applause caught me off guard. Matt came to stand by my side, and he helped me to my feet again. "Take a bow, Haley. They're all applauding for you. That was amazing."

"What's going on, Matt?" I whispered even as I took a formal bow. I guess all those theatrical productions we'd performed as kids gave me one useful skill for this moment.

"As I said, I wanted to get your performance on video where there's good acoustics. It's time for us to leave so the symphony can continue their concert."

I walked alongside him in a daze. Had that really just happened? This was the best night ever.

"You were amazing!" Mom exclaimed as she pulled me into a hug I wasn't expecting.

"When did you get here?" I asked.

"We've been here the whole evening waiting for your performance. That was absolutely stunning. Mr. Abernathy will be beyond proud of you when he sees this performance."

Mom linked her arm with mine as we left the building. Outside we got into a waiting vehicle and began driving back to the condo. "Did that really just happen? I feel like I'm going to wake up in the morning and find out all of this has been a wonderful dream."

"It's all real, babe. We love you, Haley," Matt assured me.

A smile of satisfaction lifted the corners of my mouth as I leaned against Matt's side. He really was the most romantic boyfriend anyone could ever ask for. And he was mine. I was the luckiest girl alive.

CHAPTER SEVENTEEN

My hand checked to ensure my necklace remained in its rightful place. I'd lost count of how many times I'd reassured myself of its presence. This was the same seat I'd been in yesterday, but I'd been panicking because I'd been without my lucky pendant. Today was going much better. Nothing would go wrong today.

"Haley Vallem," the nurse announced to the waiting room. This was it. They were calling me back to forever change my life. As long as all the test results were what they expected, then I'd be receiving my first dose of the trial drugs.

I stood up, running my palms down across my jeans in an attempt to rid them of their nervous moisture. I hated this part; I hated feeling out of control. Luckily, Matt seemed to sense my nerves and put his hand comfortingly on my arm. Yes, everything would go fine as long as he stayed with me.

Flanked by my mother, my boyfriend, and Charlie, I left

behind all the other hopefuls in the waiting room and followed the nurse to a different room than we'd been led to the day before. This time, the nurse had me sit on the uncomfortably high exam table.

The crinkling sound of the paper underneath me gave away my every movement. To distract from its noise, I began thrumming my heels against the base of the table. I knew this action annoyed my mother, but I was too distracted to care at the moment. Just before the doctor entered the room, my hand rose to touch the edges of my heart pendant once more.

"It's still there," Matt assured me.

"Just checking," I answered, a weak smile playing across my lips.

The door opened, and someone entered the room. The throat clearing sounded directly in front of me, in my blind spot. I had to assume this was my doctor. I wished he'd move to my side so I could actually see something of him. As it was, I could only just glimpse the outline of his feet.

"Hello, Haley. How are you feeling today?"

"Fine."

"Do you know why you're here today?"

"Yes. I'm supposed to be starting the drug trial for CLN1 treatment."

"Very good. I just needed to be sure you were clear on what we are doing today. Are you willing to participate in this study?"

"Yes."

"Good. You seemed distracted yesterday, so I wanted to make sure you were in the right frame of mind for proper consent."

"I'm sorry. I lost something very important and only just discovered it was missing when they called me in to see you." My hand automatically reached up to touch the necklace. "I promise to pay better attention today."

"Good. Good." The doctor moved away from me, and I heard the squeaking of the caster-wheels of the exam chair as he rolled it closer to us. The cushion exhaled as the doctor sat down. The noises of paper being rifled through were the only sounds in the room while we waited for the doctor to continue.

"So, Haley. I have a few questions to ask you before I give you any drugs. I see you just recovered from pneumonia. How are you feeling physically? Are you tired?"

"No. It took me a bit to recover, but I feel perfect."

"Good. So, I see you've been tested for seizures in the past. Have you experienced any since these last tests were performed?"

I shook my head.

"Okay. Well, let me tell you about the findings we've had with these drugs I'm going to give you today and what you can expect. Does that sound good?"

"Yes."

"Because Batten is a brain disease, we've formulated this drug to counteract some of the major problems stemming from Batten. Some of the changes you might notice will be a better ability to think or reason. You might also find your vision could improve.

"We've had better results with younger patients, so it'll be interesting to see what comes of your issues. You might say that your age is somewhat of an anomaly and we're anxious to see how these drugs work with your system."

"I'd be okay with better sight. There's so much I want to look at," I offered, grinning as I tried to lighten the mood.

"Yes, I bet you would. Now, on to the darker side of drug trials. I have to give you the list of problems you could encounter just so you're aware of the risks involved in partaking in this study. When I'm done, then you and your mom will sign a release permitting us to begin. Does that sound fair?"

"Yes. Although I can guess the risks, but go ahead."

"I'm sure you can. Okay, here goes…" The doctor proceeded to list off so many variations of issues; it would've taken up a whole page of fine print in one of those drug ads in a magazine.

In fact, there were so many possible issues that I began to chuckle at how ridiculous this all sounded; not that it was really a laughing matter, but I was already nervous. What can I say?

By the time he got to, 'up to and including death,' I almost sighed with relief. Nothing could possibly be said after 'death,' so I knew he'd finally gotten to the end. "Wow, that's some list."

"Yes, it's pretty extensive. Now that I've detailed everything out to you, Haley, do you understand the risks involved in beginning this drug trial? And, most importantly, do you still want to continue?"

"Yes, and yes. Where do I sign?" I held out my hands, expecting them to give me the paperwork. I heard the doctor slide some papers onto a plastic clipboard and the ting of the metal as it came down to grip the papers solidly. Once in my hand, I brought the papers up close to the side of my face so I could attempt to locate the area for me to sign. Luckily, someone had highlighted the area in pink, and I slowly signed my name in my sloppy, juvenile printing.

I held out the clipboard, and someone took it away. I heard someone else signing the document, presumably my mother. Then the doctor cleared his throat, and I heard the rattling sound of pills in a bottle. The moment I'd been waiting for stood right before me, my hands resumed their sweating, and I rubbed them against the tops of my thighs.

"Haley, I'm going to give you two of these pills right now. I want you to take two pills every twelve hours. We'd like you to stay in the area for the next twenty-four hours in case you have any adverse reactions to the drugs. After that, then you're free to travel back home."

"Should I take them with food?" I asked, the slight weight of the pills in my hand a sharp contrast to the weight of their potential results on my life.

"It doesn't seem to make much difference. Go ahead and take those right now."

A paper cup of water pressed against the edge of my other hand. Not wanting to delay the inevitable, I popped the pills in my mouth and swigged the water in almost the same motion. Now we just had to wait to see what came of it all.

ಶಿ ಯಿಶಿ ಆ

By the time we arrived back at the condo, I was feeling the first side effects of the drugs. When I stepped out of the car, my balance seemed off, and I ended up grabbing for

Matt to hold me steady. His fingers threaded with mine and I welcomed his touch. I probably leaned heavier on Charlie than I ever had before.

Once we were back in the apartment, I said, "I'm feeling a little tired. I think I'm going to go lie down for a bit." I didn't want to mention that I felt like I'd just run a marathon; my mom would have worried and hovered had I admitted that part.

"How did it go?" I heard my dad ask my mom just before I shut the bedroom door. I imagined they would be talking for quite some time while I slept. It was probably better this way; I had no interest in hearing all the details of the doctor's visit all over again. Once was definitely enough!

ഇ ൽ ര

Twenty-four hours and my only reaction had been exhaustion. Hopefully, that would subside in the next few days as my body grew used to the dosage of drugs. I certainly hoped so, because spending all my time in bed was certainly not my idea of living.

Our packed bags stood ready for our departure from the amazing condominium. Matt's aunt had come over to bid us farewell; I could hear her laughing with Matt and my dad over some sports event they all had an interest in. Leave it to Matt to discover some obscure sports fact to lure my dad into a lengthy discussion.

"It was sure nice meeting all of you," Chrissy announced.

I took that as my cue to get up from the couch where I'd

been resting. Immediately the room silenced as if my movement had been so interesting as to arrest all attention. Seconds later, Matt came to my rescue, taking my hand and leading me over to his aunt. I could smell her fancy, floral perfume.

"Thank you for everything," I said simply.

"You're so very welcome, Haley. Let's just hope this gives you everything you've ever wanted. Maybe I'll be seeing you again soon."

Matt leaned in to say, "Aunt Chrissy is trying to get me to agree to spend Christmas break with her. She's hoping you'll come with me."

I grinned, thinking this sounded like a fun trip. In all my life, I never thought I'd be planning a getaway with my boyfriend. I guess there's a first for everything. "Sounds like fun," I announced brightly.

My dad cleared his throat nervously, and added, "We'll talk about that later, Haley. Right now, we should be heading down to the car. We don't want to keep Chrissy's plane waiting forever for us. She's already gone to enough trouble for us."

"Oh, Robert, it was nothing. Really. Besides, it got my favorite nephew down here to see me. I'd say we all won on this trip. It was a pleasure meeting both you and Ruth. You've raised a very special daughter." She gave everyone hugs before she declared she had to head out to some business meeting.

ഌ ശ്ശോ ര

Sitting in the fancy airplane excited me just as much this

time as it had the last. I could get used to this kind of luxury and convenience. Not only did we avoid all of the lines and crowds of people, but I also didn't have to endure the whispers of people commenting on my blindness. Not that it bothered me much anymore, but I know Matt took exception to the rudeness and I wanted to spare him from it all.

An hour into the flight, Matt's silence finally got to me. I nudged him with my elbow and asked, "What's got your mind so busy?"

"Nothing."

"Bull. Spill." I wasn't going to let this go.

Matt sighed. "I was just thinking about that laundry-list of side effects the doctor read to us. Doesn't that scare you? It sure scared me. I almost grabbed your hand and hauled you out of there."

"To be honest; not really." I could feel Matt inhaling for a rebuttal. "No, listen. They have to outline every possible contingency, but those things only happened to a minute sample of the test subjects. They have to feel pretty confident about the drug's effectiveness, or they wouldn't risk all that research and money with a live trial."

"I guess," Matt said, sighing through the two words.

"Besides, what I'm doing is no different than what your brother's doing to further Batten research."

"My brother? Jimmy's dead and buried. What could he possibly be doing?"

"No, your mother told me they donated his body to help with the Batten research."

"What?!" Matt exclaimed. "No, they didn't! They wouldn't have done that to him!"

I tried to reach out to Matt, but he must have jumped clean out of his chair. "I'm sorry, Matt; I thought you knew. Your mom didn't make it seem like it was a secret."

"Well, she sure forgot to mention that little detail to me!"

"What's going on here," my dad interrupted.

"Nothing!" I said at the same time as Matt.

As if to prove this point, Matt resumed his seat next to me. In a harsh whisper, he said, "Tell me everything you know about this."

"Matt, think about it for a second. What your family went through might be able to be prevented if they can study what happened to your brother on a molecular level. Don't let his death be in vain."

"Listen, Haley; I get what you're saying on a logical level. I'm just angry that nobody thought it was important to tell me about it before now."

"I don't think it was a secret. Besides, I believe your brother would've wanted to do it. I know I would." My thoughts turned inward, and Matt continued to brood over my revelation. I wish I'd kept my mouth shut, but I couldn't take it back. At least Matt knew the truth now. What he did with it was up to him.

Chapter Eighteen

A small party greeted my arrival at home. I should've known my brother and sisters would want to know how things went since none of them could come with us on such short notice. Still, I could feel the drugs zapping my energy even as I stood in the doorway to the living room.

"I'm going to head home, Haley," Matt whispered into my ear just before he kissed my cheek. Before I could say anything more to him, he squeezed my hand in farewell and left my side, the screen door slamming to indicate his abrupt departure.

I wished we'd had more time to discuss the news about his brother. I hated thinking he left here mad and I certainly didn't want to trade places with his mother, either. Still, my family expected to hear about my trip, so I let Charlie know I wanted to walk over to the couch where I plunked myself down with a relieved sigh.

Even though I'd slept for most of the flight, I still felt like I could go to bed and stay there for the remainder of the night. I hoped these drugs would begin assimilating faster so I could get my life back; it seemed like such a waste to sleep through everything!

Jackson and JB flanked me on the couch, both of them eager to hear about the private jet ride. Of course, that would be the only part they heard in the whole adventure. Still, I had to agree how amazing the surprise had been, especially since going the private route was so much faster and more convenient than waiting around for commercial flights.

"Hey, did you know Matt wants to become a pilot when he's done with high school?" I asked my friends.

"No," replied JB.

"Yeah; I think I remember him saying something about it once. I didn't think he was serious, though. That's cool. Maybe he can take us up. He could learn how to do all those aerobatic tricks, and we could do loops over our houses."

"Ugh, I think I'll pass on that one," I said, my stomach flip-flopping with just the thought of it. I don't know what came over Jackson sometimes; he had the strangest sense of adventure. Maybe his unpredictability and my stability are what kept us drawn together.

The room went silent, and I frowned as I tried to figure out why. Suddenly, everyone began singing the birthday song, and I heard Rose's voice coming to a stop right in front of me. I could tell she held a birthday cake because I could feel the heat of the candles and smell the sweetness of the frosting.

Dutifully, I drew in a deep breath and blew out all the candles. My family began laughing, and Rose started coughing. I guess I must've blown the smoke right into her face; my bad. "Sorry, sis," I said, unable to prevent myself from chuckling at her expense.

"Totally my fault for being in the line of fire...or smoke, in this case, I guess," Rose sputtered through the smoke still hovering in front of her face.

After consuming copious amounts of cake and ice cream in the dining room, we returned to the living room for me to open presents. With all of the commotion on my actual birthday, I didn't really expect a celebration this year. Don't get me wrong. I loved it; except it seemed wrong to be celebrating without Matt beside me. I knew he was at home arguing with his parents over the news I dropped on him.

I tore open the packages placed in my lap and let my fingers try to figure out what everything was. Hunter had given me a gift card to buy audiobooks to add to my collection. He knew how I loved getting lost in all those great stories.

Jackson and JB had each made me friendship bracelets to match the ones they wore. I loved being part of our tight-knit group. This simple jewelry let everyone know we were a part of something together. "Plus, I want to create a special video featuring you playing your cello," Jackson announced.

I realized he hadn't been privy to Matt's surprise with my performance with the symphony. No way would I ruin his enthusiastic offer with what had already happened. Besides, Jackson always made filming the productions a fun event. If nothing else, we would have a blast for an afternoon.

Rose had found some plush pillows for my bed. She had impeccable timing since it seemed I'd be spending more time sleeping these days. I loved the different textures on them, even if I couldn't really tell what they looked like. Julia kneeled in front of me as she placed her large, rectangular package on my lap. "I knew this was for you the moment I found it. I hope you like it."

No matter what she bought me, I knew I'd love it because she had thought of me. I ripped open the paper and pulled up the lid. After sifting through several sheets of tissue paper, my fingers discovered a silky material. "What is it?"

"It's a formal dress. I thought you might be interested in going to a dance or two at school this year. Maybe with a certain someone who shall remain nameless," she teased.

"Okay, I get the idea already. Thank you, Julia. It feels amazing already. What color is it?"

"As if you'd have to ask. Of course, it's your favorite shade of lavender. Slightly more sophisticated than the pink you used to be infatuated with."

I put the package off to my side as I folded my arms around my sister's neck and hugged her. I whispered into her ear, "Now I just have to convince Matt to ask me to the dance."

"I don't see that as being a problem. You may not have, but we've all seen the way he looks at you. He's clearly smitten," Julia whispered in reply before she pulled back and stepped away. "Happy birthday, Haley."

"Thanks, sis." Out of nowhere, I began yawning. Apparently, my body finally decided to let down from the big trip, but I certainly wished to have more time with my friends and family.

"I think that's our cue to leave, JB. Are you ready?" Jackson asked suddenly. "Haley clearly needs to get more rest. I'll be back tomorrow, and we can catch up then. See you." As per his usual, he patted my head as he walked past.

"See you later, Haley. Happy birthday," JB said as he joined Jackson at the front door.

"Thanks for coming over, guys. I really like the bracelets." I held up my arm to demonstrate how they fit perfectly on my wrist. Even that casual motion felt like a herculean effort, and my hand dropped lifelessly into my lap. "I don't know why I'm so tired," I whined.

"The doctor warned us that your body would take time adjusting to the new drugs. Before you go off to bed, your dad and I wanted to tell you what we've done for your birthday."

"Oh, you guys have done enough. I mean, we just went to San Francisco, and all."

Mom sat down where Jackson had vacated the spot next to me. She took hold of my hand and answered, "That wasn't exactly a vacation. No, we know how much you love going on the houseboat, and we weren't able to make that happen this summer because we thought we'd be heading to New York.

"So, we contacted the owners of the boat, and they have it available this next week. It'd be really relaxing for you to sit out on the water and soak up the sun. What do you think?"

"Well," I started, but I didn't know how to tell her I would rather spend time with Matt.

"We've also invited Matt's family to join us, that is...if you're up for it."

"That's perfect, Mom!" I flung my arms around her as I fought back my tears of joy. The only thing troubling me was whether or not Matt and his family would want to come after the bomb I inadvertently dropped. They might be too upset with me to want to be cooped up on a boat for a week.

"Great. We'll make all the arrangements then. Why don't you head off to bed, you feel a bit chilled, and it's obvious you're tired. You've had a long day, after all. I might even consider taking a nap myself." She patted my leg lovingly.

I knew she'd never take a nap; she only said that to make me feel less self-conscious about my suddenly frail condition. Stifling another yawn, I shook my head and said, "It's too early for me to fall asleep. I have to take my second dose at eight."

"I'll make sure you take it. Don't worry. Just rest for now," Mom assured me.

I rather liked thinking she would be responsible for remembering; my thoughts kept jumbling anyway. I'm sure it was just the fatigue setting in, so I tried not to worry about it too much. Besides, the doctor said I'd be getting better mental clarity, so I just had to give it time to work.

ಬ ಡಾಬ ಡ

I'd hoped to see Matt again before the night ended, but he must've been too preoccupied with his family. Even my phone remained silent, although I'd sent him a couple of silly text messages. Still nothing. I hated the silence. I'd rather have him yelling and screaming his frustration rather than keeping everything to himself.

After my mom woke me up for my second dose, I fought off the sleep trying to take over. I listened to music played too loudly through my earbuds until I no longer felt the pull of exhaustion as the drugs shifted into the next phase.

The doctor had said it was important to analyze the progress of the drug's interactions with my body. As far as I was concerned, I was merely being scientific at this point. Maybe I should video record myself to get proper documentation.

After the drowsiness wore off, I felt a strange numbing sensation in my fingertips, and my thoughts seemed to race at lightning speed. I'm not sure this was what the doctor meant by clarity; it was more confusing than anything. So much passed through my mind, it almost made me dizzy and thankful I was already reclined on my bed with my new pillows.

I'm not sure how much time passed; it felt like nothing. Something didn't seem quite right, but I couldn't pinpoint what it was so I dismissed it immediately. Rather than dwell on it, I decided it was too late for Matt to make an appearance or even to call, so I took out my earbuds and rolled over to sleep for the night.

Charlie took up his regular spot against my side. I loved having him with me; it reminded me of when I was little, and another dog used to sleep with me. Those were simpler times when I still dreamed of becoming a ballerina or an actress one day after I grew up. I'm pretty sure I fell asleep with a grin on my face with this thought fresh on my mind.

CHAPTER NINETEEN

No! It couldn't be lost, not after all this time! Immediately my hand rose to my neck, my fingers searching vainly for the pendant I knew was lost. Only, my fingers brushed against the familiar nick in the side. How can this be? I know it was lost.

I rolled over and sat up in bed, my hand still clasping the precious pendant as if my life depended on it. "Oh, thank goodness! It was only a dream," I whispered out loud.

"What happened, Haley?" Matt asked, his hand reaching out to touch my arm.

I about jumped to the ceiling with fright. "When did you get here?" I asked defensively.

"A while ago. It looked like you had a bad dream. Do you want to talk about it?"

I laced my fingers with his, taking comfort in his presence. "I was afraid you wouldn't come back after..." I stuttered to a stop, not wanting to remind him of a hurtful subject.

"Don't worry, Haley. I worked out everything with my

parents. Hey; they told me the good news about the houseboat. It sounds like a lot of fun. Doesn't it?"

"The houseboat," I repeated, my mind trying to put together what he was talking about. Suddenly, it all clicked together like the final piece of a puzzle. "Yes. We go every year. Does this mean you and your parents are going to come with us? I don't want to go if you aren't with me."

"Nothing will keep me away, Haley. Besides, I'm dying to see you waterskiing. After all of your boasting, I need proof that you actually can do it."

"I don't think I'll be attempting it this year. I've been a little tired lately if you hadn't noticed."

Matt squeezed my hand playfully. "Likely story. I'll find out the truth at some point. I guess we'll just have to laze around in our skimpy bathing suits and soak up the sun. I'm not opposed to that either."

I chuckled at his lame attempt at humor. Just as I started to move off my bed to freshen up in the bathroom, everything seemed to go off-kilter. Even my hearing seemed like my head was under water, nothing made sense.

"Haley! Haley! What's going on?" Matt asked, his body pressed against mine as I curled up against his chest.

I limply pushed my hand against his torso as I leveraged myself away from him. "I'm fine, Matt. I just got dizzy. It's just the medication. Don't worry so much; I'm fine."

"That didn't seem fine to me, Haley. We should tell your parents about it at least." Matt shifted off of the bed, his hand still lightly resting on my shoulder.

As fast as I could manage, my hand reached out and grasped his wrist before he could move. "No!" I urgently whispered. "My mother will totally overreact; she'll probably rush me down to the hospital to have a battery of tests run. I just got dizzy, Matt. Please. Just keep this between us."

"Has this happened before?"

I didn't like Matt's tone, but I wasn't going to lie to him. Shaking my head, I replied, "Not like that. Last night when I first lay down, it felt like I had vertigo. It didn't last very long, and then I slept great."

"Okay, here's what we'll do. You tell me about every episode and how long it lasts. If I think it's getting worse, then I'll talk to your parents. Agreed?"

I let go of his wrist, pulling my arms around my middle to hug myself in self-defense. How did this all get so out of control? "It doesn't sound like I have much choice."

"Nope. I love you, Haley. I just want to keep you safe."

"I've got to go to the bathroom," I declared, pushing my legs over the side of the bed and walking confidently across the room. I hoped my progress looked normal because my head felt as if it were swirling again. This had better pass soon because I couldn't live with it forever.

No sooner had I reached the bathroom sink, than I had to grip the countertop to keep myself from falling onto the floor. The next thing I knew, my knees crashed down onto the tile floor, but my hands kept their hold on the counter. I don't know how long I kneeled there, but Matt's rapid knocking on the door brought me back to the present.

"Haley! If you don't open this door in the next five seconds, I'm coming in there," he threatened.

Somehow I managed to pull myself off the floor and open the door just in time. Matt must have seen something which scared him because he immediately crushed me to his chest. "Haley, you're not okay. You're as pale as a ghost. We need to tell your parents."

"Please don't, Matt. I just stood up too fast. Can you help me get back to bed?" I only meant for him to guide me back, but he had other ideas. I flailed, a squeal of surprise erupting from my lips, when he swept me off my feet, cradling me like a little child, and strode back to my bedside in seconds.

No sooner had we made it back when my mother entered my bedroom. "What's going on?" she asked instantly.

"Nothing," I replied.

"I just helped her get back into bed," Matt said at the same time.

"Hmm. I brought Haley her morning dose."

My hand shot out to take them from her, hoping she'd give them to me and leave right away. Unfortunately, she had other ideas as she gave me the medication and seated herself at the end of my mattress. "How are you feeling today, Haley? Do you have any more energy?"

"Not really," I mumbled, hastily downing the pills with a swig of water. "Did you get the houseboat arranged? Matt just told me his family's coming."

"Yes. I think it'll be a good distraction from everything before you head back to school." She tweaked my toes playfully like she had done when I was little.

Nodding, I couldn't agree more, I thought with a smile. Turning my attention back to Matt, I said, "I missed you at my birthday party yesterday."

"Yeah, I probably should've stayed a little longer, but I didn't have my gift for you with me anyway. Are you ready to open it now?"

"What? Of course!" I held out my hands, eager to discover what he might have gotten me. "I can't believe you got me something more. You already did so much for me on my actual birthday." In the middle of my palm, I felt a small box without much weight at all. "What is it?" I asked, suddenly nervous.

"Well, you always seem so surprised that I want to hang out with you, so I thought I'd get you something so you'd know exactly what my intentions were for you. Open it."

With trembling fingers, I managed to pull the small amount of paper from the outside of the box. I could feel a hinge on the back and cracked open the case. With the sunlight pouring into my room right over my bed, I shifted my position so I could hold the box up into my peripheral vision. A small, gold band stood inside a crevice of black velvet. "Matt!"

"This is a promise ring, Haley. I promise to keep myself for you and you only until you're ready. I love you, Haley." He took the box from my lax grip and plucked out the ring. "I'd like you to wear this on your necklace so it'll be near your heart."

"Okay," I replied, my hands instantly finding the clasp on my delicate chain and unfastening it. I held it out to Matt and held my breath while he threaded the ring onto the necklace.

Rather than hand it back to me, he brushed my hair to the side and settled it back onto my neck for me. I loved the idea of the two items sharing a space on my chest; they both represented a love I had in my life. The difference in the weight seemed odd at first, but I knew I'd get used to it in short order.

My finger caressed the ring, tracing its circular shape in wonder. I wished it could have taken its place on my hand, preferably a particular finger on my left hand, but that would have to wait at least another year before it would be a consideration. "I love it, Matt. Thank you."

I felt his hand caressing my arm; then everything went strange again with my world shifting off-kilter. This could not be happening at this most beautiful moment in my life, yet I was powerless to stop it. Even the ringing in my ears made it impossible to hear what was being said to me.

ಖಿ ಲತಿಖಿ ಲ

Something seemed off when I came back to my normal awareness. Caressing the rough linen under my fingertips, I knew this could not be my bed at home. A sick feeling struck me, instantly confirmed by my inhaling the antiseptic smell of a hospital.

"What happened?" I asked mostly to myself, not knowing if I were alone.

"You blacked out, Haley. We brought you to the emergency room," Matt replied, his hand warming a spot on my shoulder as he stood by the head of the bed.

"No! I don't want to be here. Take me home, please."

"We didn't have much choice when you remained unresponsive. Your mom was afraid you were having a seizure."

"Did I?"

"No. They did some sort of test, and they were able to confirm you just had low blood pressure and not a seizure."

Matt's fingers rubbed against my shoulder, tapping out a rhythm I almost recognized.

"Thank goodness," my mom sighed, as she entered the room. "You're finally awake. How're you feeling?"

"Fine. Please, Mom, take me home. I don't want to be here. I just need to get something to eat, and I'll feel perfect again." This was what I had tried to avoid. I hated hospitals, tests, and feeling confined. Moreover, I hated making my family worry about me. Mom's next words set all my worries aside and allowed me to breathe freely once again.

"The doctors have cleared you to go. Matt, if you could step out, I'll get Haley dressed, and then we can all leave."

I could hear the crinkling of a plastic bag, which I assumed carried my personal belongings. They really should have something more personable than a glorified shopping bag for their patients.

As soon as I heard the door click shut, I asked, "How long was I out? I don't remember anything beyond when Matt gave me…" Instantly alarmed, I wondered if I might have imagined the whole promise ring thing. My hand flew up to my neck where I discovered the ring did exist. With a sigh of relief, I continued, "the ring."

"Drink this," my mom said as she picked up my hand where she placed a metal can. "It's guava nectar and should help you to have more energy. I already opened it and put in a straw to make it easier for you."

"Thanks, Mom," I said, hastily bringing it up to my lips and taking a long swig of the sweet juice. I hoped it would kick in fast so I could assist her in getting me dressed. The last thing I needed was for her to see how weak I'd suddenly become and then hover even more than usual.

A few minutes later, I found myself dressed and seated in a wheelchair. Nurse Taylor patted my shoulder familiarly as she wheeled me to the exit. "We've got to stop meeting like this, Haley," she teased.

"I'll do what I can," I replied with a low chuckle. "This isn't your usual ward."

"No, but I heard you were here and requested the honor of handling your discharge."

"Thanks, I appreciate it." Only then did I realize someone was missing. I really was off my game for it to have taken this long. Feeling slightly alarmed, I asked, "Where's Charlie?"

"We left him at home with your brother," Mom answered swiftly.

"Oh. I'm sorry I scared everyone."

"It's not your fault," Mom said. Then changing the subject, she added, "The doctor advised us to make sure you had more frequent meals so your blood sugar would remain constant until you get used to your new medication."

"That makes sense," I agreed, fervently hoping this would be the solution to my growing problems. When the wheelchair bumped over the threshold, the jarring motion caused me to jump more than I usually would have reacted.

Only then did I notice how much easier it was to see out of my peripheral vision. Maybe the light shone brighter outside or possibly even wishful thinking on my part, considering I'd only been taking the new medication for three days, but I could swear I already saw better.

If my vision could begin to recover this fast, maybe

there was hope for the rest of me after all. I'd keep this little nugget of information to myself, so I wouldn't get anyone's hopes up if it turned out to be inaccurate.

CHAPTER TWENTY

Rather than staying confined to my bedroom, I set up shop on the living room couch so I could be near the family's action. Although I preferred the lighting in my bedroom, I used this opportunity to gauge the improvement in my eyesight. It had improved, even if only marginally. I'd take it!

Charlie's multiple attempts to smother me on the couch finally gave way to him deciding to curl up immediately below me on the floor. My hand dangled over the edge, brushing against the top of his head to let him know I still loved him. Every once in a while, he'd lick my fingers, probably to get a reaction out of me.

A long time ago, I'd discovered my family hovered over me less outside of my bedroom. Being bedridden must really change how people thought about me, so I'd avoid that area as much as I could. Besides, it was more entertaining with the television broadcasting game shows in the background.

Finishing up her phone calls for the day, Mom joined me

on the couch. Sitting near my feet, she lifted them onto her lap and massaged them just the way I liked. "How are you feeling?"

The dreaded question, but one I patiently answered, "Fine." I could mouth the next one without even being able to see her.

"Are you hungry?"

I gestured over to the empty plate on the coffee table, "Jackson brought a sandwich for me when he came."

"But that was almost two hours ago. Let me get you some juice." Mom jumped up from the couch and rushed to the kitchen. I could hear every move she made, but I turned my face so I could attempt to watch her as well. The images remained blurry, but I could definitely see her, even at this distance.

I took the glass and dutifully drank as she resumed her seat. I held the glass with both hands and let it rest on my belly. "What's going to happen to my foundation once I'm done with the drug trials?"

"Haley, we won't stop the fight until no mother has to endure the pain of losing her child to this dreaded disease."

"I figured as much. What about after I leave the house?"

"Where are you going?" she asked, her tone slightly higher as she tried to contain her worry.

"Not right away, but eventually I plan on leaving." My hand went up to the ring, and I added, "Maybe I'll get married and start a family of my own. Or, if not a family, at least I'll have my husband and Charlie."

"Oh, I don't know. There's so much to do for the foundation; it's a full-time job, you know."

"Yes, but you need to do something to relax and have

fun. Both of you deserve some time away, where you can unwind from all this stress. Maybe you should take a cruise to Hawaii or something."

"That sounds nice." She tweaked my toe playfully and started to say something else when the phone rang. With a longsuffering sigh, she said, "Duty calls. I'll be back in a bit."

I rested my head against the back of the couch, letting my mind wander aimlessly. Something felt wrong inside me, but I couldn't say anything about it until I identified the source. Anyone would immediately point to the drugs and say they caused it, but I knew differently.

No, this stemmed from something else; something I probably should have mentioned to the doctor before accepting the drug trial. I had too many blank spots in my memory, almost as if I'd experienced long blackouts; maybe even as I slept. I don't think the episode in front of Matt and my mom was the first incidence.

෩ ෩෩ ෩

Well, that went downhill quickly. Mom and Dad were out in the hallway arguing with the doctor, and I experienced a sense of déjà vu as I felt the cold liquid dripping from the IV into my arm. Two days of intensive care after my massive seizure and the doctor was advising my mother to stop the drug trial.

"It's her only chance of living!" she argued.

"It's probably the cause of her seizures. We need to wean her off of the drugs. I've already contacted the doctor in charge of the study, and he agrees with me. Haley was their oldest test subject, and she's proven not to be an ideal test subject."

"How dare you! You had no right to interfere."

"It's the safest course for Haley. I'm sorry, Mrs. Vallem, but Haley has been dropped from the trial."

"I'm sorry," Matt whispered to me from my bedside.

"Did you already know?" I asked, turning my attention away from the hallway and back to my boyfriend.

"I suspected it'd come to this. You weren't the same after you started the new regimen. To be honest, it really scared me."

"I'm sorry, Matt."

"What's even worse is the room they put you."

"Why's that?"

"This's where my brother…" he faltered.

I didn't want to hear him finish. I rushed to fill the silence, "Oh, that's terrible! Well, I'm getting out of here soon; don't worry about that!" I felt a shiver run through me at the idea of Jimmy drawing his last labored breath in this room. My fingers curled into Charlie's warm fur as I breathed a sigh of relief that they'd allowed him to come and be with me. I'm sure Charlie provided the turning point for my recovery.

"I guess this unplanned stay in the hospital is going to put an end to the houseboat trip," I said, my voice low and sad at the lost opportunity.

"Yeah, but I've got something cool planned for us instead when you get home." He squeezed my hand.

I'm pretty sure he was only making that up to entice me to get well enough to actually come home. "I love you," I said, taking us both by surprise, although it truly came from my heart. He leaned over the bed and gently kissed my lips. As soon as he pulled away, I whispered, "I want to go home today. Do you think it's possible?"

※ ✿ ✿

Two days later, the doctors finally allowed me to leave. For once, I welcomed the familiarity of my bedroom where I could luxuriate in the comfort of my own bed. My family and friends made regular rounds to ensure my every need was taken care of.

In the rare moments where I found myself alone, thoughts of my mortality kept plaguing me. Repeatedly, my thoughts kept returning to my closet where I could make out my purple dress hanging prominently. Would I soon be wearing it again?

"Hey, are you ready for your surprise, Haley?" Matt brightly asked from the doorway.

Plastering a smile on my face, I nodded enthusiastically and replied, "You bet!"

He came to my bedside, taking a seat on the edge, and dropped a small package on my stomach. "You'll never guess what it is."

I felt the size of the container, and said, "It feels like a CD. Am I right?"

Matt chuckled, amused at my uncanny ability to guess accurately. "Yes. But what's on it is the big surprise."

I opened the container and held it out to him, before asking, "Can you put it in my CD player then?"

"Sure thing." He took it from me and left the bed. Seconds later, the beautiful music of an orchestra filled the room. "Do you recognize it?"

"No, should I?" I cocked my head to the side and let the music flow through me. Even if it didn't ring any bells, I could still appreciate the skill of the players. One song ended and a cello soloist began. The notes resonated within my mind. This was my song. No, this was me playing my song. "Matt! Where'd you get this?"

"The symphony just delivered it. Isn't it amazing, Haley? Your music has been sent out to thousands of the symphony fans. You're famous!"

He hugged me to him, and I felt tears of joy falling from my eyes. This truly was a special gift from him, bigger than I could have imagined for myself.

"There's more," Matt added, pulling away. "We just broke a new record on YouTube views with this same video."

"How many views? Two hundred thousand?" I picked the most outlandish number I could think of.

"Try three million views. Haley, it's going viral and only getting bigger by the day!"

"Wow! I bet Jackson's going out of his mind!" I laughed at the idea of how far my friend had come with his video channel.

"I'll say, he called me at two in the morning to announce we'd reached the one million mark."

"Sounds about right."

"Oh, and the owner of the orchestra sent you a personal invitation to come and play with them again any time you're in town. How about that?" Matt pulled out an envelope from his coat pocket and handed it over to me.

"Wow; I won't be able to stop Mr. Abernathy from gloating about this. He always insisted I'd make it big with my music if I'd just apply myself a little more to practice." We laughed together, the music continuing to play, the perfect scene we created only marred by my lack of energy to move away from my bed.

CHAPTER TWENTY-ONE

This bedrest bit was getting pretty old, only made tolerable by Matt's almost continual company. He kept teasing me that I had to get better soon because school was starting up again next week and he didn't want to go alone. Matt had an uncanny ability to make me laugh at the dumbest things.

I might not have been so melancholy had the weather been normal for the season. But the rain poured down outside my window for the fifth straight day. Maybe my blindness caused me to be more susceptible to the change in barometric pressure. I should have lived in Arizona where I could soak up the rays every day. Sunshine always made everything better.

"I'm pretty sure this isn't how you planned on spending your summer," I grumbled as soon as Jackson left us alone for the afternoon.

Jackson had offered to go to the school to get all of our locker assignments as well as picking up our class schedules. He usually arranged for us to be in the same classes so he could be my guide throughout the day. This time, he would make sure Matt had at least one class the same.

"You mean sitting at my girlfriend's bedside? No, that was actually better than my original plans. Although, we all thought we'd be taking care of Jimmy, but that turned out quite different."

My thrill at hearing him call me his girlfriend was promptly overshadowed by my guilt. "I'm sorry for bringing it up, Matt. That was really insensitive of me." I swiftly thought of how to turn his thoughts of his brother into something positive.

"You once told me you had a lot of things planned to do with your brother when he got better. We did some of them this summer, but I'm sure there were more things. Right?"

He absently played with my fingers with both of his hands. It seemed so strange that such casual contact could cause me to feel so loved and cherished. He took a minute before answering.

"Sure. He loved petting zoos and wanted to visit one in every state. Then there was his weird fascination with bugs and spiders. I'm pretty sure he would have become an entomologist if he'd had the chance. He even wanted to start a worm farm and sell the poop as fertilizer."

"Okay, that's a little strange." I chuckled as I imagined how we would have accomplished this bucket list item for our video series. Shaking my head in dismissal, I added, "I'm glad we skipped doing that this summer, to be honest. Where'd he come up with that idea? Wasn't he a little young for something so advanced?"

"He was really smart; besides, I think they did a field

trip about it on Sesame Street or something. Ever since then, we'd catch him hiding worms in plastic cups in his room."

"Ugh! Your poor mom. At least he didn't put them in his pockets!"

"Oh, he did that, too. She finally started making my dad go through Jimmy's pockets before she would do the laundry. Obviously, that was before his diagnosis and before he went blind."

Even though I was smiling, I felt empty inside, like my fire had been extinguished. I was sure it was just the lingering effects of the drugs, but it still felt weird. Trying to bring myself out of it, I said, "I've been working on a bucket list."

"Oh yeah? Let's see it."

I tapped my forehead and answered, "I've kept it all in here. I didn't want Mom or Hunter to find it and think I was planning on dying or anything drastic like that."

"That makes sense. How about you tell me what you've got planned, and I can see about what we can get done together. I'm sure some of the things are group activities, right?"

"Sure. To start with, there's skydiving. I've always thought that would be the next level up after zip-lining. I've always wanted to fly and be free like the birds. It probably stems from feeling cooped up inside all the time."

I'm sure Matt thought he was being stealthy, but I could hear his pen rolling across the paper he held. I didn't say anything to stop him; it was probably better to have it written down. After all, my bucket list wasn't complete.

"What else?"

"Hang-gliding."

"Definitely noticing a trend here."

"You asked. Okay, then there's going up in a hot-air balloon. I've heard there's no wind when you're in the basket because you're traveling at the same speed as the air itself. I want to feel that."

"Do you have anything you want to do on the ground?"

"Sure. Let me think, how about visiting all seven of the natural wonders of the world."

"Why? I mean, I don't mean to be rude, Haley; but why would you want to go there? You can't even see it."

I sighed, rolling my head until I faced Matt. "There's more to our senses than just sight. It's fun to hear what people are saying around me about what they see. And I want to smell it all. Sometimes, I wish I could bottle up the scents from where we've gone so I could open it up and relive the adventure when I'm stuck at home on rainy days like today.

"You know, like the time we went to the coast and we got caught out in the thunder and lightning storm. I love that ozone smell mixed with the salty spray of the sea. There's nothing else like it in the world, but I can imagine it vividly even now."

"Okay, I stand corrected. When you describe it like that, I know what you're talking about." More scribbling sounded before he asked, "What else do you want to do?"

It seemed like hours passed as we talked about our plans for the future. I know I told him more than I actually meant to and I thought of things while he was there that hadn't been on the list before. Having him by my side made me want to accomplish more.

"That's all I remember right now, but I'll be sure to keep you updated when I think of more." I stifled a yawn, my hand came up to cover my mouth. My fingers had started shaking lately, which I detested because it demonstrated a physical symptom for people to notice and make comments about.

"I hate this, Haley! It just isn't fair!" Matt spoke angrily, his hand grabbing mine to hold it steady.

His outburst caught me by surprise and I jumped in alarm. Out of reflex, my other hand grabbed the pendant on my chest, feeling surprised to find the addition of Matt's ring nestled next to the familiar heart pendant. As soon as I calmed myself, I said, "Hey, it's okay, Matt. It's just the drugs leaving my system."

"How can you even say that? How is any of what you've gone through okay with you?" His fingers dug into my palm as he got angrier.

I weakly squeezed his fingers and sighed. My movement must have reminded him of his hold on me because he relaxed his hand until it became pleasant again. Matt's patience had run out and I needed to say something to help give him some comfort. "I heard something once that made a lot of sense."

"What's that?" Matt rested his elbows on the mattress as he leaned in closer to me. I could feel the heat radiating off of his skin.

"That we choose to come into this life for certain experiences."

"What do you mean? Like reincarnation or something?"

"No, not exactly. It's more meaningful than that; it's like this existence is merely the rift in our reality. There's more to life than just what we do here on Earth."

"No! I refuse to believe anyone would choose a life of suffering and pain. Nobody comes here wanting to die as a kid."

"But look at all of the beauty and love I've known. People go their whole lives and don't ever find what I've had with you and my family and friends. I've been so blessed and I'm thankful for all of it, even the bad stuff, because it made the good things feel so much…more. Do you understand what I'm saying?"

"I hear what you're saying; but that doesn't mean I agree with it."

"Well, it's easier for me to accept my reality if I think I chose it rather than the idea of having some random mishap decide to pick me for trouble." I yawned again, only this time I didn't try to hide it. "You know what? I'm getting pretty tired. I think I'm going to take a nap. We can talk about this again tomorrow. Okay?"

"Sure. I love you, Haley," Matt spoke before leaning over and softly kissing my lips. His fingers caressed my cheek and I brought my hand up to cover his.

I'm sure my eyes were facing him, but I couldn't see him as I answered, "You're the best thing to ever happen in my life. Your love and friendship was the one thing on my bucket list that I never thought I'd have. I love you, too, Matt."

"And I'll keep on loving you forever, Haley. Sleep well. Tomorrow's supposed to be sunny and I plan on taking you outside to soak up the sunshine."

A smile played on my lips as I said, "Sounds like a dream after all this unseasonable rain we've had. See you tomorrow." My lips tingled where he'd kissed me, and I could still feel the warmth of his touch on my cheek. I pulled the covers up higher as a chill coursed through my body as soon as Matt moved away from me.

Charlie immediately jumped up on the bed and took up his usual spot next to me as soon as Matt left. His body snuggled next to my leg and side, warming me instantly. His chin rested across my ribcage and I took comfort in stroking the silky hair on his head. "Stay with me, Charlie. I always feel safer when you're near."

I listened as Matt left my room and heard the faint click of my bedroom door latching shut. I still had something I wanted to do tonight and I wanted to make sure I had enough strength to finish before it got too late.

I reached over and picked up the video camera which I kept there for these occasions. I pushed the record button and began speaking. "Hunter, when you get the chance, I'd like you to write out this note and keep it in a special place until the time is right. You'll know when that is."

I'm not sure how long it took for me to get everything recorded, my mind kept wandering in longer and longer lapses in between thoughts. Still, I'm fairly certain I remembered the gist of what I wanted to be said.

I don't remember if I turned off the recording or not, but my hand relaxed enough for it to fall onto the bed beside me. I'd pick it up in the morning, it seemed like too much effort right now.

My thoughts raced lightning fast and I wondered if this were one of the side-effects the doctors had warned me about. It reminded me of the old days when I could still see the movies at the theater. Reaching up, my fingers touched my pendant while I gave into the motions of the pictures in my head, delighting in my own personal show.

CHAPTER TWENTY-TWO
(MATT)

If it weren't for the silk lining and the flowers surrounding her, Matt could easily imagine she just slept. Just like how he'd found her that fateful morning in her bedroom, she seemed so peaceful. The moment he realized she was gone would be forever burned into his brain.

As promised, he'd walked to her house bright and early, enjoying the warm sunshine along the way. He'd greeted her mother in the usual manner of waving as he passed her while she conducted foundation business at the dining table.

"Are you taking her out for a picnic?" she asked brightly as she hung up the phone.

He stopped to turn around, his hand going up to the plaid blanket slung over his shoulder while his fingers tightened their grip on the picnic basket. "Yep. Has she eaten breakfast yet?"

"No. The last time I looked in on her, she was still asleep."

"Good. I brought all her favorites for breakfast. I'm so glad the sunshine decided to return today, she needs cheering up."

"I agree," Ruth said, turning her attention back to business as the phone rang.

With a spring to his step, he looked forward to seeing her surprise with what he'd brought. Standing in her doorway, he loved seeing how Charlie snuggled with her, his muzzle resting on her chest. "Haley, it's time to wake up."

He stepped into the room, slowly realizing something was off. Even Charlie didn't move to acknowledge his entrance. Dropping the basket and the blanket, he sprinted across the room and grabbed Haley's hand where it rested on the dog's shoulder.

Instantly, he knew the truth, but he refused to give it a place in his mind. "Haley!" he yelled, knowing it was useless. Charlie whimpered his sorrow as Matt pushed him aside so he could attempt to give Haley CPR.

Everything else seemed like a blur after that. From Ruth screaming and crying to Hunter calling an ambulance, there wasn't a single quiet moment for quite some time. The autopsy found she had suffered a grand mal seizure and passed away sometime in the middle of the night.

Charlie kept his vigil as he stepped up next to her casket. This was something he had been unable to do with his brother. Looking down at Haley, his vision blurred with tears as he realized this would be his last time ever being with her physically.

He hoped she had been right about her spirit living on with this life's experience. Maybe she was watching him even still. A tear dripped down his cheek and fell onto her arm.

She looked beautiful in her lavender dress. It was the same one she'd worn to his brother's memorial service. The same one her mother said she wore to all the funerals they'd attended. It only seemed fitting she would wear it to her own.

"Where's her necklace?" Matt asked, suddenly noticing her bare neckline.

Ruth cleared her throat and held out her hand. "She wanted you to have it," she said, the pendant and ring resting in her palm.

He wanted to run away from the gesture if only to deny that it was happening. Still, his hand moved of its own accord and accepted the gift. Without hesitating, he unthreaded the promise ring and placed it on Haley's left hand. "It's where it would have gone eventually," he whispered before turning away for the last time.

Jackson stood behind him, ready to give his respects to the family. Matt held out the pendant and said, "You should have this. It was your gift to her; she treasured it and you more than you'll ever know."

Shaking his head, Jackson refused to accept the offer. "No, it was her last wish for you to have it. I'm not about to go against her now; I was never able to deny her anything."

֍ ⊱⊰ ֍

After the service at the cemetery, Charlie became Matt's shadow. It was almost as if he knew his service with Haley had finished and now he needed to be there for Matt. Even now, sitting in the Vallem's living room, Charlie sat at Matt's feet where he stood next to the fireplace.

Hunter cleared his throat to get everyone's attention. "Thanks for coming to our family meeting, Matt. Haley wanted me to tell everyone a few things after her service."

"What? When did she talk about this with you," Ruth asked, her expression lined with pain at her daughter's acknowledgment that this day would come.

"The first time was a long time ago, but she talked to me about it last week as well. Anyway, she wanted me to give you this." Hunter held out a letter to his mother. "She asked me to write this out for her in the last video she made the night she died." His voice choked up on the last word.

Ruth took the paper from her son; her eyes already blurry with tears. She wiped the moisture away and sniffed deeply before she began reading the words aloud:

> I had originally planned on writing individual letters to each of you, but I decided I'd end up repeating myself. What comes to my mind most often is how incredibly lucky I was to have you in my life. I've learned so much in such a short amount of time; it'd be impossible for me to write it all here.
>
> So, Hunter has been working with me on a special project. He's going to give you each a flash drive. Ever since my diagnosis, Hunter and I have been working together on this special video project, documenting my journey and thoughts along the way.

Please don't be mad at Hunter for keeping it a secret. Also, please understand his desire to see this project through before going off to college. He never wanted to disappoint you, but he always wanted to be here with me until my end. He's the best brother ever!

Anyway, before you start crying too much to be able to read this still, I wanted to share some of my insights:

First, people spend too much time trying to 'see' the world, and not nearly enough time trying to understand it. I was so blessed to lose my sight so I could see more clearly with my other senses. I've come to understand how much we need one another in order to truly be happy.

Second, I may not have lived a long life, but I've loved the life I've lived. My family is amazing, strong, generous, resilient, and happy. We've experienced so much together, growing and learning along the way.

Third, the greatest possession of my life is the relationships I encountered and the love I've felt. I was once told we come into this world to live out a certain experience we haven't felt before. If this is true, then I'm truly blessed with the deep, abiding, and selfless acts of love I've encountered.

I know it's hard to hear this right now, but please don't be sad for me. I've lived every minute I was given, and I want you to learn to find the same happiness that I have. Treasure our memories together, and go out and create more in my memory.

Live your life. Find love in everything. And most of all, share your happiness with the world.

The room remained silent except for the sniffles of people unsuccessfully attempting to hold back their tears. This was Haley's last gift to the family, and they were truly touched. Ruth's hands dropped as she came to the final words and asked, "Where are the flash drives she spoke about?"

"Right here," Hunter answered, holding out his hand containing nine small figurines. "She picked out a different theme for each person." He handed the rose to his sister, Rose, a roller skate for Julia, a football for their dad, a heart for their mom, a dragon for himself, a camera for Jackson, a police shield for JB, a book for Jay, and an airplane for Matt.

"She had me compile certain moments for each person which she thought would make great memories for you. Some of them are repeated on different drives if you were all there together, but each one has her own style.

"She even had me record special songs she wrote for each of you. That's the first thing you'll find on each of your copies."

Robert spoke up, "When did you two have time for all of this?"

"Contrary to popular belief, I wasn't always playing video games late into the night," Hunter defended himself, a rueful smile playing on his lips.

"I should probably head home now," Matt spoke up. He hugged everyone as he made his way across the room; Charlie dogging his heels the whole way. When he got to the front door, he tried to let himself out while holding Charlie back.

"No, Matt. Charlie needs to go with you. He was your dog first, after all."

"I can't take him; you guys need him."

Ruth came over and kneeled next to Charlie. She stroked the dog's head affectionately and looked up at Matt. "He wants to be with you, Matt. There's no way we would ever deny him or you of the chance to stay together."

She pushed the door open, and Charlie bolted over to Matt's side, his eyes eagerly awaiting Matt's next command. "See? Thank you for coming today, Matt. Don't be a stranger, okay? You're like family now, you know."

"Thanks, Mrs. Vallem." Matt turned away, Charlie ran circles around him, eager to be going home again. With this unexpected gift, an idea formed in Matt's head about what he would do next. In a day or two, he'd contact Jackson and see if he were up to the challenge.

Epilogue
(Thirteen Months Later)

Standing at the monument indicating the border between Washington and Canada, and also marking the end of the 2,650-mile trail, Matt brought his hand up to Haley's pendant dangling from its original chain around his neck. He never went anywhere without it, and he could feel Haley's spirit surrounding him as he worked his way through her bucket list.

Turning around, he gave a thumbs-up signal to Jackson who had his camera trained on him. "This completes the Pacific Crest Trail for you, Haley," he announced. He pulled out a sheet of paper and made quite the show of checking off the sixth item on her bucket list.

Just then, Charlie jumped up like he needed to see what Matt was doing. As always, Haley's dog accompanied him on this quest to complete the bucket list. He completed the team, taking in the sights, enjoying the journey, and sharing their travels with the world.

"What's next, Charlie? Do you want to go skydiving, or do you want to sit that one out? Huh, boy?" Matt ruffled the hair on Charlie's head as he affectionately talked with him. The two had become inseparable since Haley passed. Matt often wondered if this were something Haley had planned from the moment they'd discovered Charlie's past. After all, she had always insisted that Matt should spend as much time with the big dog as he could.

Jackson finished his panoramic shot of their final location before he put the camera in his backpack and came to stand beside Matt and Charlie. "That sure did take longer than I expected."

"Yeah, five amazing months, but it was worth it."

"I think my YouTube subscribers are going to love it."

"Definitely. Especially that part where the rain washed out that whole section of the trail, and we had to repel to get around it. Although, it would've been better if you hadn't been screaming like a girl for the first five minutes."

"Hey, that was terrifying." Jackson grimaced at the memory, thankful to be alive to tell the tale.

"But we did it. We finished the first column of tasks on Haley's list."

"It's too bad we have to take a break from this project just because of school. It'd be awesome if we could just skip the real life and keep working on the list."

"I think our parents would have different ideas. We were lucky they let us out of school early to start this." They fell silent as they absorbed the gentle quietness of the wooded landscape. As they'd learned from Haley, they closed their eyes and soaked in the serenity of their surroundings. After hearing Jackson's stomach growl for the third time, Matt said, "We should probably eat while we're waiting."

They wearily sat down with their backs resting against the border marker, almost too tired to dig out their food from the backpacks. Today, they would break out a special meal, saved for the occasions when they finished one of Haley's dreams.

"Do you know what I've been thinking about?" Jackson asked as he held out the opened bag of M&M's toward Matt.

He grabbed out a handful of the peanut treats and said, "I can only imagine. Hopefully, it involves something with a comfortable place to sleep."

"Man, we are spending too much time together. I was thinking it'd be really amazing to spend the night in my own bed soon."

They paused their conversation to watch a small airplane fly overhead until the trees blocked their view. Matt sighed and turned his attention back to the peanut butter and jelly sandwich he held in his other hand.

"Are you still working on getting your pilot's license?" Jackson asked.

"Yeah, I'm almost ready to take the written exam."

"How many flight hours do you have?"

"Only thirty-five, but that's all with an instructor. I'll need a lot more after that to get where I need."

"You know, Haley really wanted you to become a pilot for Angel Flight West. It's all she talked about for days."

"Yeah. That's why I've got to get 250 pilot-in-command hours before I can even apply. Luckily, my aunt has offered to sponsor my training. Otherwise, I'd never be able to afford it on my own. What about you? Any grand plans?"

"Nah, I'll know more after I graduate from film school." Jackson popped the rest of his sandwich into his mouth and slapped his hands against his jeans. A plume of dust flew away, causing Jackson to think twice about repeating the motion. "I'm sure something amazing will come along, though."

"I agree. I think this documentary we're filming will open doors for you, at least."

"I hope so. Speaking of which; are you ready to head down to the main road and see if our ride has shown up yet?"

Together, the boys and Charlie trekked down the path with more energy than they'd felt in a long time. Just knowing they'd completed the journey left them feeling a major sense of accomplishment. They rounded the last corner and spotted Hunter leaning against the side of a rental car.

"You're a sight for sore eyes!" Jackson called out.

"Yeah, I was getting mighty tired of only seeing Jackson," Matt teased, playfully jabbing Jackson in the shoulder. The pair had formed quite the friendship during their time together, one which would last a lifetime.

Hunter opted to give them each a handshake after taking in their grubby attire. "Maybe we'll drive with the windows down. When was the last time either of you bothered to bathe?"

The boys looked at one another, then shrugged dismissively. "After how freezing that last lake turned out to be, we decided it wasn't that important after all."

"Yeah, I thought I'd bite my tongue off from shivering so hard," Jackson added as he flung his backpack into the trunk of the car before getting into the front seat.

Matt and Charlie took their spots across the back seat. It felt good to have someone taking care of them for a change. The air blowing in the windows as they drove down the highway reminded Matt of Haley's love for flying. His fingers touched the heart-shaped pendant in the same manner he'd seen her do innumerable times.

No sooner had they started driving when Hunter declared, "We're stopping at the first place with a bathroom so you two can get cleaned up. You guys stink!" The faster they drove, the better it became, especially with all the windows down.

Hunter glanced at Matt through the rearview mirror. "I think you guys picked the hardest thing on Haley's list. Do you think you'll be ready for the next adventure?"

"Absolutely!" Jackson declared, already forgetting their recent hardships.

"Bring it on!" Matt stated at the same time as Jackson. Charlie barked as the boys all laughed, causing them to laugh harder. Matt pulled Charlie closer, rubbing his side affectionately, more thankful than ever that he could share this journey with a dog and people who meant so much to Haley.

Want to Help?
Find out more at...

Haley's Heroes Foundation

 Call 503-580-1736
 m.me/curebattendisease
 haleysheroes@givingback.org
 https://haleysheroesfoundation.org

To keep updated on the next book to be written by Amy Proebstel, visit www.AmyProebstel.com.

Receive a FREE exclusive novella, ***Tuala's Lost Boy: Ceren's Story*** by signing up for Amy Proebstel's newsletter.

GET MY FREE NOVELLA NOW
at http://bit.ly/BMNLSignUp

You can also follow Amy Proebstel on Facebook at www.facebook.com/levelsofascension.

ABOUT THE AUTHOR

Amy is a native Oregonian and she enjoys the quiet of living in the countryside with her husband, Richard, and their daughter, Kailey. She shares her life and house with four Pomeranians and a special cat who thinks she's a dog.

Reading and writing books has always been a passion in her life. There's nothing better than getting pulled into other people's journeys, feeling their emotions, and enjoying their successes. She writes when she's inspired, usually after midnight, and the results have been fun to watch unfold as she immerses herself in the world of her characters.

This book refers to Haley's Heroes Foundation which is a real foundation set up by the Pollman family to find a cure for Batten disease for which their 9-year-old daughter, Haley, was diagnosed in 2017, and is already legally blind. At this point, Batten disease is rare, incurable, and fatal within 10 years of diagnosis.

The progression of symptoms include: blindness, muscle

immobility, seizures, dementia, and death. Go to https://geni.us/Haleys_Heroes to find out how you can help with funding this important research. Children's lives literally depend on your support.

Don't want to donate directly? When you buy ***The Rift In Our Reality***, which follows an older version of Haley who is navigating her teenage years while fighting for her life, half of the proceeds of this Sweet Young Adult Medical Romance will go directly to the Haley's Heroes Foundation to help find the cure Haley so desperately needs.

Feel free to email Amy at Amy@LevelsofAscension.com.

Billionaire's Venture Romance Series

A Cowboy's Recipe for Romance
Loving Texas Tea
Properties of Love (coming Summer 2019)
Plane Love (coming Summer 2019)
Capitalizing on Love (coming Summer 2019)
Ether of Love (coming Summer 2019)

Romances Beyond Tuala Trilogy

An Agent For Love
The Missing Love Link
An Undimensional Love Story

Levels of Ascension, Urban Fantasy Series

Outside Ascension
Inside Ascension
Ascension Quest
Ascension's Call
Answering Ascension
Ascension Seekers
Ascension's Lure
Above Ascension
Between Ascension (coming Summer 2019)
Ascension's Gate (coming Fall 2019)
Ruling Ascension (coming Winter 2020)
Ascension Watchers (coming Spring 2020)
Ascension's Truth (coming Summer 2020)

Box Sets
Ascension Discovery – Box Set, Books 1-4
Ascension's Prophecy – Box Set, Books 5-7

A Sweet Young Adult Medical Romance

The Rift In Our Reality

Made in the USA
San Bernardino, CA
08 May 2019